Where There Is Love

Where There Is Love

Linda Becker

Seeker Publishing
2014

First Printing: 2014

ISBN 978-0-578-14256-2

Seeker Publishing

O'Fallon MO

Preface

Is it possible for there to be something so unique in this world as two souls who are meant to be together forever? Over the span of my short lifetime I have become very cynical and tend to believe this idea only exists in our imaginations. Then again, perhaps we are able to imagine it only because it is real but so extremely rare that most of us only dream of it and never experience it.

If we only believed in what we ourselves experienced our universe would be quite empty, would it not? Where would we be without our dreams and hopes of something greater than ourselves? What is it that binds us all together in this life? Do we not spend our entire lives searching for that thing— that one thing—that makes life worth living? And could that thing simply be…love? With that kind of power, could love transcend time and space, life and death? Was John Lennon right when he said, "All You Need Is Love?" Could love be all there is?

I do not have the answers to all of those questions. However, I'm convinced that love is a very powerful energy. Just how far its strength reaches, I'm not sure. I do know that it forced me to write this story.

> *"Though I speak with the tongues of men and of angels, but have not love, I have become sounding brass or a clanging cymbal. And though I have the gift of prophecy, and understand all mysteries and all knowledge, and though I have all faith, so that I could remove mountains, but have not love, I am nothing. And though I bestow all my goods to feed the poor, and though I give my body to be burned, but have not love, it profits me nothing." Corinthians 13:1-3*

1

If ever two souls were meant to be together it was those of Helen and David. It is very rare for those souls to find each other at such a young age and recognize it so easily, but it was true of them. From the very moment that Helen met David, they were virtually inseparable—both physically and emotionally. There was something between them that could not be explained. Not that either of them ever needed an explanation. Because they had been together since they were babies, neither of them knew what life was like without the other.

Helen and David might never have met if it hadn't been for one fateful afternoon at the local coffee shop. Helen's mother, Cathy, was pregnant with Helen and was just leaving the shop after visiting with her circle of friends. Joan—who was pregnant with David and who belonged to no such similar circle—was having coffee alone. As Cathy began to pass by Joan's table, the glint of a silver heart pendant around her neck caught Cathy's eye. Cathy thought about dismissing her observation and continuing on, but something told her to turn around and speak to Joan.

"Excuse me, but I couldn't help notice the pendant you were wearing. I have the exact same one. See?" Cathy pulled her necklace out from under the neckline of her sweater.

Joan, being caught completely off-guard, looked immediately at the pendant Cathy was holding between her fingers. "Oh my! It most certainly is the same!" she said. Joan's fingers went up to grasp her own silver heart-shaped pendant. It was solid silver with a raised filigree pattern and tiny pearl in the center—somewhat unusual—and now strangely common in this little coffee shop. Joan invited Cathy to sit down, and they shared how each had come by their jewelries. Joan's father had given it to her on her sixteenth birthday. It had been his mother's, and when she had no daughters to pass it onto, it became his. Cathy's mother had given the necklace to her for a graduation gift. Her mother never told her where it came from, but just that it was very special and she should save it for her own daughter.

The two women both noted how strange it was that they came from different areas of the country and would end up with identical necklaces. Cathy had been born and raised in Mississippi, but Joan came from Virginia. As they chatted they realized that they had more in common than a piece of jewelry. For one thing, they were both expecting their first child in the same month. It also turned out that they lived only a few blocks from each other. In fact, by the time they finished their conversation, they were surprised that they hadn't met much sooner. It was the beginning of a friendship that would last many years and create the opportunity for Helen and David to find each other.

After their children were born, Cathy and Joan continued to see each other regularly and so their babies grew up together. Helen was a striking red-headed, green-eyed girl. There was no hiding her Irish ancestry in her looks or her behavior. She was energetic, loving, and stubborn to the core. David was a blonde-haired, blue-eyed, and fair-skinned little boy. He was quiet, and there was a calmness about him that seemed unusual for a boy his age, but it didn't stop him from laughing with delight as he and Helen played. They complemented each other well. They looked like a couple of cherubs from a Renaissance painting, frolicking together in the park while their mothers looked on.

As they grew older and were able to get around without their mothers, Helen and David still went everywhere together. They were classmates at school, and their summers were filled with adventures as far as their little imaginations would take them. The two would run through the grassy fields behind their houses, laughing, pretending to be wild horses or two hunters lost in the jungles of Africa. On rainy days they got into their "boat" and sailed to a beautiful place known as "David's Island." David was the king of the island and Helen was his fair maiden. David would fight off imaginary dragons with his cardboard sword, and then rescue Lady Helen from the shackles of the Evil Queen. These were Helen's favorite days. She loved when it was just the two of them in their own world and nothing else existed except them.

The games they played as children were replaced with more grown up activities as they entered their teenage years. They swam, rode bicycles, and went hiking through the woodlands of central Mississippi. Although the games had changed, their love for each other did not. In fact, their imaginary world called "David's Island" only became more real to them. It was not a place they would go, but a virtual world—cut off from everyone else's idea of reality—that very much existed in their minds. He would always be her king, and she would always be his lady.

In the summer of their eleventh year, Helen and David had just finished a long hike to the river. They pulled off their sneakers to dip their sweaty bare feet into the cool flowing water. With feet in the water, both leaned back on their elbows to look up at the soft blue sky. Helen pulled the rubber band out of her long, curly, red hair and shook her head to let it fall loosely around her shoulders and then lay back down on the cool grass. David lay back next to her and took her hand in his.

"David, will we always be together?" asked Helen. She'd asked him that question a million times, but she kept asking him. It made her feel so good to hear his answer. It had almost become another game for them, and it gave Helen the opportunity to imagine their life together in the future, which always made her smile.

"Yes, Helen. We will always be together," David would say patiently.

"But what if my parents move us away? How will you find me?"

"I will look everywhere for you, Helen. I won't rest until I find you," said David.

Helen wiped the sweat from her forehead. She paused for a moment trying to think of another situation that she could spring on him. She wrinkled up her freckled nose as she pondered her next question, and then she asked, "What if I was captured by pirates, and they took me on their ship, and sailed to the other side of the world, and hid me away in the deepest, darkest caves? How would you find me? How can you be so sure that we would be together?"

David took a deep breath and turned his face away from the warm sun to look at Helen. He raised himself up on one hand. Helen turned to face him. His deep blue eyes looked into hers and said, "Helen, you would just have to sit still, close your eyes, and think of me, and I would turn the universe inside out to find you. I would go anywhere and fight anything to get to you—witches, dragons, and even pirates. If I have to pass through a hundred lifetimes, I will do it to find you. I may be an old man and you may be an old woman. You may not even recognize me by the time it happens, but you will know and I will know, because nothing can separate us. We will always be together. I promise you. Now stop worrying." He rolled onto his back. His eyes squinted in the bright sunlight as he put his hands behind his head to cushion the hard earth beneath it.

His serious stare slightly frightened Helen. She'd never heard him answer her with such complete reassurance. In fact, she wasn't completely sure she understood all of it, but he'd convinced her that she had nothing to fear. She liked the way he looked just then—so strong. She turned her head back again to face the sky. She closed her eyes and smiled as she kicked up the river water with her right foot. "Thank you, God, for David," she whispered very quietly to herself.

While their souls were fully compatible, Helen—as an individual—was really nothing like David, and David was nothing like Helen. They came from different backgrounds and did not share the same kind of home life. Helen's father was a doctor. Her mother had been a schoolteacher until she met Helen's father. The family of three lived in a very well-kept brick two-story house in an upper middle-class neighborhood in Jackson, Mississippi. David's father was a banker. He and his parents lived just a few blocks away in a more modest house but still in a respectable part of town. David's mother had never held a job. She had met her husband when she was seventeen and he was nineteen. Despite his young age, David's father was ambitious. He had started as a teller at the bank but had risen quickly into management.

While Helen's parents were deeply devoted to each other and their lives revolved around making the best life for Helen that they could, David's parents were very different. David's mother, Joan, was

a very loving mother. But his father, Henry, was quite the opposite. When David was very young, Henry was drafted into the army. He had served overseas during the war in Europe. When he returned, there was a noticeable change in him. He was quiet, moody and—
at times—became violent. Joan was devastated by his new behavior. She remembered the sweet kind young boy she married, but David was too young to remember him that way. It broke her heart to know that David would never see his father as anyone other than this dark individual who was in a constant struggle with his demons.

To the outside world David's father was a respectable, responsible, model citizen. But inside David's home, Henry's dark side often showed itself to Joan and David. These outbursts usually resulted in bruises on Joan's arms or David's back. None of this was ever talked about outside of their household, but Helen knew. She had seen David's bruises in the summer when they would go swimming. She knew, but she never said a word. She knew one day they would run away together where his father couldn't find David, but until that time, she prayed that God would find a way to keep David safe so he couldn't be hurt anymore.

Very little changes came as David and Helen grew older. At the age of fourteen, the two were even closer than ever. Helen was becoming a young woman and experiencing all the changes— physically and emotionally—that come with womanhood. David was lagging behind her a little in the physical development. He was no longer taller than Helen. Not that it mattered to either one of them.

Helen's mother wished her daughter would dress more like a lady and act less like a boy. As a compromise, Helen would wear dresses with sneakers, so she could keep up with David while still looking like a girl. Their cherubic days of childhood were behind them. Now they looked more like a couple from the comics with their obvious differences in height and development.

As David grew older he was facing other challenges that most young men never have to encounter. It was getting more and more difficult to deal with his father's physical abuse of his mother. He could stand a beating or two from the man, but he couldn't bear to watch his mother be hurt by someone much larger and stronger than she was. The tension was building inside their home. It wouldn't be long before a full-fledged conflict would break out amongst them. David knew this. He was afraid—afraid to rise up and defy the commandment to honor his father. But he was also angry and tired of seeing his mother living in a frightened world. He was tired of watching her be humiliated and hurt while he stood by and did nothing.

The long sunny days of summer ended too quickly, and autumn was demanding to take over. Before they knew it, October was upon them. Gone were the innocent days of freedom. Even though October came every year to extinguish what was left of summer, the fall of 1954 seemed different. This year everything seemed to take on more meaning. The death of summer felt deeper this time—as if it threatened to never return as it always had after the spring. David and Helen both felt this new gravity taking over their childhood days, but neither could quite understand it as anything more than a puzzling, dark sensation.

Halloween had been a very warm day, but now the wind was growing stronger as the night fell. Helen was dressed as Tom Sawyer—her favorite Mark Twain character. Her freckled face peered out from under a straw hat as she stood on David's front porch waiting for him to answer the door. He wore an old top hat and black cape. His mother had drawn a curly mustache on his face and he was suddenly a magician! The two were not looking to play tricks on their neighbors that night. Sensing that they were growing out of the dress up phase, they were contented to walk the dark streets and watch the children play in their costumes.

The usual bonfire had been canceled given the high winds and they ended up down at the corner soda shop to indulge in some chocolate milkshakes. Helen noisily drained the shake from her glass and giggled at how unladylike she was behaving. As much as she hated to leave her reckless childhood days behind her, she was optimistic about becoming an adult. She dreamt of the day when she and David would be married. They would have a beautiful house far away from David's father. The house would be filled with games, music and laughter from their two boys, two girls and the two of them. It was going to be a wonderful life. She smiled gleefully at David as he slowly savored his last few sips.

It was a school night, which meant an early bedtime. David walked Helen home. Reluctantly she said goodnight. She hated for it all to end. The air was filled with electricity, and she felt like it was a night when just about anything could happen. Just before he turned to leave, he took Helen's hand in his, pressed it to his lips and kissed it gently. He looked up at her and said, "Goodnight, Lady Helen, until we meet again."

She smiled at his theatrical farewell and replied very dramatically, "Goodnight my king." David turned away and cut a path through her backyard for a shortcut home. As he disappeared into the darkness, she felt the magic go with him. She stood there watching him go as she held the back of her hand to her lips, where he had placed his just moments before. When he was no longer in sight, she sighed and trudged up her front steps, sad to see the last of the warm evenings end and dreading the impending doom of winter.

A storm blew up just at bedtime. Helen was shivering under her covers as the wind howled outside. With each gust, the shingles flapped, the walls moaned slightly, and the tips of the tree branches rapped on the glass of her bedroom window. The dry leaves scuttled across the pavement, formed a gang that hit the side of the house, and then tried their best to fly as high as possible against the brick wall before surrendering to the ground. Occasionally one or two made it all the way up to become stuck in the gutter. The soft flashes of light in the distance had now increased to loud strikes that lit up her room even when her eyes were closed. Helen tried her best to cover her eyes and ears with her pillow. She had always been terribly afraid of storms ever since she could remember. She hated the sound of thunder, and it was horrific that evening. It was as if the demons from all their Halloween adventures had been unleashed at once on them. She thought about how happy she had been earlier that night—how carefree and easy. Now everything seemed dark and scary. Her imagination was taking over and making her more frightened as she envisioned the trees becoming monsters, attempting to break through the glass and enter her room.

A knock on her window pane startled her. She lifted her head out from under the covers to see what it was, but all she could see from her bed was the rain running down the glass. She climbed out of bed to get a closer look and prayed that she wouldn't see a monster at the window. She was relieved when she saw that it was David. He'd scaled the tree and was hanging on for dear life while he tapped at her window. She went over and lifted the pane for him to come inside. She was so thankful to see him. Always her hero, he had heard the storm come up just as he was going to bed and rushed to be with her.

When they were younger and had been out playing near the river a storm had blown up and caught them both out in the open with raging winds, strong downpours, and terrible lightning. Helen became hysterical while hiding under a tree. David held onto her tightly and promised her everything would be alright. But it was no use. Her fear was so great. She continued to sob wildly, so he just held her tightly until the storm passed. She never forgot that afternoon or how patient and calm he had been as he sheltered her from the danger. David never forgot the frightened look on her face and promised he would never leave her to be alone and afraid again.

After David entered the room he ordered Helen to get back in bed and under the covers. He lay down next to her on the bed as close as he could get.

"David, you're shivering. Get under the covers with me," she said.

He leaned over and kissed her on the cheek. "I'm okay. Besides it wouldn't be right, Helen. I'll warm up soon. I'll stay here until you fall asleep."

Lightning struck and the thunder clapped loudly, shaking the house. "David, I'm scared," she whispered in the dark. She reached her hand over to find his and clasped it tightly.

"It's okay, Helen. I'll protect you," he whispered back. His hand squeezed her hand back.

"David, promise you'll always be here when I'm afraid."

"I promise, Helen. I'll always be here," he said.

"And we'll always be together?"

"I promise, Lady Helen. We will be together forever. Close your eyes now and stop worrying. You don't ever have to be afraid." He stroked her hair lightly with his fingers. She closed her eyes and breathed deeply, trying to relax. It felt warm with him lying so close to her. She felt safe and she could finally rest. *What would I do without you, David?* She quickly drifted off to sleep. When Helen awoke in the morning, David was gone. She ate breakfast, brushed her teeth, combed her hair and left for school. Usually David would meet her along the way to school, but not today. She was surprised when he wasn't in class either. School was wasted on her that day, for she could think of nothing else but David. She sat there staring out the window wondering what would keep him away. She thought about the night before and how comforting it was to lie next to him while the storm raged outside. It was so hard to stay focused on anything her teacher was saying and she was never so thankful for the last bell of the day to ring.

She arrived home quickly and out of breath. The air had that first chill to it that nobody is really ready for, and she had run to avoid being out in it any longer than she needed. The house was dark when she walked inside. The fall season meant shorter days and it was already apparent that the change was occurring. She looked around for her mother and found her sitting quietly in the living room, staring out the window.

"Mother, I'm going over to David's house. He wasn't in school today and I want to see if he's okay."

"Helen," her mother turned to look at her. "Wait. I have to tell you something. Come in and sit down."

Cathy's eyes were bloodshot and her cheeks tear-stained. Helen became a little nervous as worrisome thoughts clouded her mind. She slowly walked into the room and hesitantly sat down on the sofa. All the windows in the house were open. Fresh autumn air drifted through the room and past Helen's nose. She thought she detected a slight wintery smell, and it made her shiver. It had been an incredibly beautiful day with clear skies and sunshine, but now clouds were gathering. Helen could feel a change all around her. She could tell something terrible had happened. Her thoughts quickly turned to her father, and tears began to well in her eyes as she imagined losing him. She carefully swallowed and tried to prepare herself for the worst as her mother began to speak.

"Helen, I've had some rather bad news." Cathy began with what she thought was a strong approach, but her voice soon began quivering as she continued. The tears began to flow down her already tear-stained face, and she nearly choked trying to relate the horrible story to her daughter. Helen watched as Cathy struggled to explain how David had gone home last night to find his drunken father out of control and strangling his mother on the kitchen floor. David rushed to help his mother by pulling his father off of her. In the end, David saved his mother's life, but lost his own. Now Joan was in the hospital and Henry was in the city jail for murder.

Helen couldn't recall much more than that as she slowly walked up the stairs to her room. She forced her feet to rise up and meet each new step as her mind reeled from the information her mother had just given to her. The shock had erased the memory of her eyes rolling back in her head, her hysterical outbreak, the screams of disbelief, and uncontrollable sobbing. Only her mother would remember how Helen ran to her and started flailing her arms, and crying out, "No! That's not true! You're lying! It's not true!" Helen continued to scream at her mother as if she could change the outcome of the news by her rampage. Cathy held her tightly in her arms and didn't say a word while Helen wore herself out. When she could no longer fight the reality she was facing, she pulled free from her mother's arms and left the room.

She lay on her bed until it was dark, past her father's return from work, through supper and bath time. She lay there in the darkness staring out the window at the moon, wondering how she could ever care about anything ever again. Her thoughts raced through her mind at lightning speed. The tears poured from her eyes and down her face onto her very wet pillowcase. "David, you promised that you'd never leave me. You said we would be together forever. Where are you? I need you. I need you, David."

Helen quieted herself as she waited for an answer to come. In the silence memories of David's words came back to her and forced her to think more clearly. *I'll just be still and wait here*, she thought to herself. *He told me to be still and wait and he would come for me.* "I'll be still, David," she whispered in a trembling voice. "Come back for me. I'll wait for you. Just, please, please come back for me." She closed her eyes and begged God that this day never happened, and she would wake in the morning to find it had been a bad dream.

2

Armed with only the clothes she was wearing and her life savings that amounted to eighty dollars, Julie hitchhiked her way from Tennessee to just outside Jacksonville, Florida. She tried to keep her nose pointed out the window as much as she could that afternoon to avoid the terrible stench coming from her driver who was in desperate need of a bath. When he finally pulled in to a small truck stop off of the interstate, she was grateful to climb out of his cab. She offered to pay him for the ride, but he told her to keep it. She looked around the dusty little town and she sighed. She was eighteen, on her own, no job, and her money was dwindling rapidly. She would have to find some work for a little while before she could move on, but first she had to eat. She made her way across the parking lot to the little truck stop diner.

Julie was a beautiful blonde-haired, brown-eyed girl born into a quiet Southern household. There was no affection shown between her mother and father or any shown toward her that she could recall in the eighteen years she'd lived with them. She rarely remembered seeing her father as she was growing up. He was either at work or at the neighborhood tavern getting drunk. When he came home it was late and he usually went straight to bed without dinner. Her mother didn't seem to mind. She kept busy with the typical chores of cleaning, cooking, sewing, and shopping. There was barely a word spoken between them.

Much of Julie's social time as a small child was spent with her imaginary friends—a well-loved stuffed bunny, a doll whose hair was missing in a few places due to a bad haircut experience, and a sock monkey made by her grandmother. Although her world had many voids, it was the only world Julie had ever known, so she had no comparisons and no conscious longing for anything more.

As Julie began to develop into a young woman and mix with others at school, something awakened in her that she never knew existed. She noticed that boys liked the way she looked and the more attention she showed them, the more she received in return. She enjoyed the admiration and soon realized that it was very crucial to keep it coming. She began to dress in ways that flattered her figure, so that she would be noticed. But flirting and come hither glances weren't all that the boys wanted from her. In order to maintain the level of affection and attention she desired, she would have to give a little more in return. She started "dating" boys after school. Sometimes they would go to the park and find a grove of trees to hide in while they made out. Sometimes she would invite a boy to her basement where she would let him feel her naked breasts and kiss her with an open mouth. She found it necessary to give away more and more of her body in order to maintain their level of interest and her level of need. Whatever it took, it was worth it to her.

She lost her virginity at fifteen to a boy of eighteen with white-blonde hair and devilish blue eyes whom she met after school in the soda shop. He looked at her as if he could see right through her. He told her how beautiful she was and how much he'd like to take her out on a date if only she was a little older. He told her she looked like she was seventeen, which was exactly what she wanted to hear. They never even got out of the parking lot. She laid herself down in the back seat of his car and let him pull off her panties. From there it went pretty fast and, in the end, left her feeling a little disappointed. But it opened up for her a new fascination with sex and how to find love and acceptance.

With very little parental guidance or supervision, it was easy for her to get out of the house and stay out on almost any given night. The girls in her class had very little respect for her and the boys the same age bored her, so she hung out with an older crowd. Being exceptionally bright, she was able to skim through high school without paying much attention or studying. She partied with all the right people who could get her pot, beer and sex.

Just days before her eighteenth birthday, Julie's father died of pancreatic cancer. It had been a horrific eight months since his diagnosis, watching him deteriorate and suffer. Despite the fact that he had not been much of a father, she loved him and it was hard to let him go. She didn't blame him for staying away from home and drinking as much as he did. She didn't see any reason for him to come home to such emptiness. Why would he? She resented her mother for being so emotionally vacant to them both, and she blamed her for forcing them to endure a lonely existence. Hours after her father's body was buried in the ground, Julie left home to find a place where she could belong.

The truck stop was a typical greasy spoon operation. It smelled of smoke, old grease, and pancake syrup. Julie sat down in a booth and looked over the menu. As she mulled over her choices, she noticed a man watching her from across the room. He tried to hide the fact that he was watching her, but to Julie it was very obvious. She knew when a man was scoping her out. She'd had advanced training in it. While she was eating her burger and fries, she watched him sipping his coffee and moving his eyes over the room to get another glance at her. She was used to men watching her all the time, but this guy was different. Something about him made her want to watch him too. He was very cute. She wanted to get a better look at him, but she didn't want him to see her eyeing him back. She placed her menu out in front of her face, so she could stare at him while it looked like she was just reading. It worked until the waitress came over to take her order.

While Julie was just finishing her hamburger and fries, she saw him pay his bill. He stood up and looked as if he was going to walk over to her table. Julie licked her lips and brushed her fingers through her straight wind-blown hair in a half attempt to comb it. She lowered her head to try and sniff for odors. The last thing she wanted was to smell like that last truck driver she'd been with, but when she raised her eyes expecting to see him standing in front of her, he was gone. The front door slammed shut. She looked out the window to see him walking away. Julie watched him walk through the parking lot to the sidewalk. His long, brown, wavy hair was blowing in the breeze along with the fringe on his suede jacket. She liked the way his butt looked in his faded bell bottom jeans, and she thought he was the coolest guy she'd ever seen. She assumed that she hadn't impressed him given his quick exit. She decided to turn her focus on her short-term future. It would be dark soon and she had no place to stay and very little cash.

The waitress came over and stood in front of her as she totaled up Julie's dinner ticket. Her dyed black hair was pulled up tightly into a bun so severely that it only accentuated her pale and deeply lined face. The name tag on her tan polyester tweed uniform read, "Beverly." Julie watched Beverly's thin painted red lips move in a circle as she chewed her gum. They stopped revolving only for a moment to say, "Will that be all, hon?" Then they continued to rotate.

"Yeah," Julie said and reached up to take the check from her. Then she added, "Hey, Beverly, you don't know anyone that's hiring, do you?"

The waitress looked down her nose at Julie, chewed on her gum, and said, "We had a waitress quit last week. You can check with Frank in the kitchen and see if he wants to hire you. You're awful young, honey. You sure you can handle these truckers? They can get pretty hardcore sometimes."

Julie smiled. "Trust me. I know how to handle any kind of guy."

"Yeah, I imagine you've had to deal with a few from the looks of you," said Beverly without the slightest bit of a smile. "Let's go back and talk to Frank."

An hour later Julie was walking out the door with a tan polyester tweed waitress uniform and apron. Beverly told her about a motel down the road that would rent to her by the week, if she mentioned her name to the owner. That would give her a little time to find a more permanent place to live. All Julie cared about right now though was knocking off two days' worth of road dust and sleeping in a real bed. Feeling completely drained, she slept soundly that night despite the noise from the highway. She didn't wake up until noon.

She was to start work on the dinner shift, which was usually a bit slower than breakfast and lunch. It would be easier for her to train during the evenings. She brushed her hair back into a ponytail and stood back to admire herself in her new uniform. She thought she looked ghastly, but it was a job, and that's all that mattered at the moment. She was on her way to making a life for herself and she was excited.

Her first night on the job was hectic. For a slow shift, it was quite busy and confusing for Julie. She tried her best to keep up with everything Beverly was telling her and tried not to cry when Frank barked at her. "Don't pay no attention to him, hon. He just don't know any other way to be. He's a sexually frustrated old man with nothing better to do than agitate everyone around him." Beverly smiled a big red-lipped smile and then went back to chewing her gum.

As things slowed down, Beverly told Julie to handle a table on her own. There was a single man sitting in the corner booth, so Julie walked up to him and asked if she could get him something to drink. The man looked up at her. Julie recognized him right away. It was the same man from the day before...Mr. Cool. She immediately looked back at her note pad, hoping he couldn't see her blushing, and waited for his response. The man ordered a cup of coffee, and Julie quickly whirled away to get it. She didn't know why she felt so embarrassed. It wasn't like he could read her mind and know all the indecent thoughts she'd been thinking about him the day before. Or could he?

She returned with the coffee and set it on the table. She held up her pad and pencil and asked, "Can I take your order?"

The man looked up from the menu and this time looked her right in the eyes. "Hey, didn't I see you in here yesterday?" he asked.

Julie laughed nervously. Maybe it was his pale green eyes that turned down ever so slightly in the corners. Maybe it was his long, brown, wavy hair that fell across his shoulders. Maybe it was the light brown hairs of his mustache that brushed his upper lip as he spoke and made her think about kissing him. She studied each part of him, trying to discern just what about this man made her heart pound so loudly that she was sure he could hear it. She thought it was best just to ignore her feelings and escape as quickly as possible. "Yep, that was me," she said to do her best impression of a disinterested waitress. "I just got into town. Now I'm working here. Are you ready to order?"

He gave her his order, and she walked away. The night went on in an ordinary fashion. One by one the customers left, but he stayed, continuing to sip his coffee as he had done the night before. It was just a few minutes before closing time, and he was still there. At the coaxing of Beverly, she grabbed a broom and began sweeping around his table as a way of letting him know it was time to leave. She glanced over at him while she swept. He seemed to be completely unaware of his surroundings while he carefully studied the pages in a book entitled, *The Complete Works of Monet.*

Without taking his eyes off of the book he asked, "So, where are you from?"

Quite surprised that he was even aware she was there, Julie turned around quickly to look at him. "Me?" she asked. "Tennessee," she replied.

"Hmmm…never been up there," he said. He closed the book and set it down. "Is it nice?"

"Yeah," she said. "I guess it's pretty nice."

"Then why'd you leave?" he asked. His lips turned up in a slight smirk and his eyes twinkled at her.

Julie smiled. She was finding it very difficult to resist him. "Long story," she said.

He invited her to sit down at the booth with him and she did, glancing back toward the kitchen to see if Beverly was watching. Before she knew it she was telling him her life story, and he was telling her his. Beverly yelled out from the kitchen that Julie could leave for the night, so they both got up and headed for the door. As they stepped outside, he asked her if she wanted to get a beer and talk some more. Julie agreed. They bought a six-pack at the gas station and walked to the park. Sitting on the swings of the playground, they both shared their stories of what led them to where they were now.

His name was Danny. He was an artist, but he'd had no formal training. He and his parents could not afford college, so he'd been drafted into the army and ended up doing a tour in Vietnam. He was wounded by shrapnel in his left shoulder and sent home. When he arrived back in Houston he married his high school sweetheart. Times were tough. He still held hope that someday he could sell his artwork in a gallery, but until that lucky break happened, he had to support a family. He had two children to feed, and he'd been laid off from his factory job for six months. When a friend told him he could hitch a ride to Florida and make some quick cash, he jumped at the chance. It was just a temporary job. He'd be gone in a week.

After a few hours and a few drinks, Julie knew more about Danny than she'd known about her own father. They sat on the top of a picnic table finishing the last of the beer. Danny was telling her a joke that made her laugh, and she realized that she couldn't remember the last time she had laughed at anything so hard. She'd also never spent this much time in conversation with anyone. It was so easy to be with him.

She was still giggling when she noticed Danny looking seriously at her. "You're gonna think I'm coming on to you or something, but I just gotta say you are absolutely beautiful." He stared at her as the moonlight cascaded down her long golden hair. She smiled. "I really mean it," he continued. "You're stunning. That's why I couldn't take my eyes off of you yesterday in the diner. I'd really like to sketch you…that is…if you would let me." He laughed. "That probably sounds like a line, huh? I'm really serious though. What do you think?"

"Sure. I guess," she said and took another swig of beer from her bottle. She didn't know how to handle his attention to her. Normally she could play off a guy's cheap come-ons easily, but she sensed he was seriously interested in her. It was unique and a little frightening. She hadn't realized how close they were sitting to each other until now. Her thigh was gently pressing against his, and she could feel the heat coming from him. His face was very close to hers as he continued to study her features. Julie began to study his face also. Danny had a gentle look about him and she could just sense his tenderness. That's what made him most attractive to her. She wanted so badly to say, "I think you're beautiful too." But she kept silent and watched him watching her. His lips were so close and she imagined how soft they would feel when he kissed her. Her heart was pounding, and her body was on fire with anticipation. Just then, Danny pulled away abruptly. "It's getting late. I'll walk you home." Disappointed, she threw her empty beer bottle at the trash can and stepped down from the picnic table. They walked down the street to her motel engaging in idle chit-chat to fill up the silence between them. When they finally arrived at her motel room door, she unlocked it and stepped inside the threshold.

She leaned against the corner of the doorway and said, "Thanks for the beer. I had a really good time."

Danny rested on the door frame with his left hand. "Yeah?" he asked as he bent his arm so that his face was closer to hers. "Me too," he said, smiling. He was studying her face until his eyes landed on her mouth. She could smell the beer on his breath and she wondered if he was pondering kissing her as much as she was. Without moving away he closed his eyes and said, "Do you have any idea how hard it is to leave you right now?" His mouth was so close to hers that she could almost feel his mustache tickling her lips as he spoke.

Do you know how much I want you to stay? Julie felt the heat run through her body as they both stood there waiting. She knew he wanted her and she wanted him. She couldn't let him walk away any more than he wanted to. Finally she found the courage to say quietly, "Who said you had to leave?" He opened his eyes and stared directly into hers. He leaned his face in closer and pressed his lips on her mouth very gently. For a few moments they just teased each other by barely making contact, savoring the softness of their lips' slightest touch and taking in each other's breath. The teasing turned to full-fledged passion as his tongue found her open and willing mouth.

They backed into the room and shut the door. Julie continued to lead him toward her bed as she unzipped her uniform and kicked off her shoes. Together they unbuttoned Danny's shirt. She sat down on the bed while he unfastened his belt and dropped his jeans to the floor revealing a fully erect penis in front of her face. Julie took it in both her hands and wrapped her lips around the tip. She slid her hands around his hips to his butt and pushed him deeper inside her mouth. He very willingly moved in rhythm to let it slide in and out of her warm wet mouth. His hands reached around her back and unhooked her bra. She lay back on the bed and pulled herself further on to it, so he could climb on top of her. He pulled her panties off her long silky legs and spread them apart so he could enter her. It was everything she imagined sex should be. This wasn't like the teenage sex she'd had before. He made love like a man. She could tell that he wanted to make sure that she enjoyed it as much as he did. And enjoy it, she did. They made love until neither could stay awake. Then they fell asleep in each other's arms. Just as the sun was coming up, Danny carefully kissed her so not to wake her and then tiptoed out the door.

For the next few nights, Danny would show up at the diner to eat his dinner and wait for Julie to get off work. It was like having a steady boyfriend, which was something Julie had never had. The ugly truth was that he was married and it wouldn't last. He would be gone soon and that made her heart sick. Danny had indicated that the relationship with his wife had soured many years ago. They had dated all through high school and then Danny was drafted. He promised he would marry her when he got back from Vietnam, so when he returned he felt compelled to honor his commitment. They were both very young and caught up in their parents' excitement over the wedding that they forgot to make sure they still wanted to spend forever together. The ceremony went on as planned. She was pregnant before they knew it, and there was just no going back. Another kid later and a few years down the road, she confessed to Danny that there had been someone else she was seeing while he was in Vietnam. She was confused about her feelings for Danny and the other guy. Then he lost his job, and it was everything they could do just to keep their household together. There just wasn't time to think about feelings or emotions. They were in survival mode.

Julie listened to Danny tell his story and it frustrated her. On one hand she felt sorry for his marriage to be in such turmoil. On the other hand, she wished he would give up on his wife and stay with her. But Danny wasn't the kind of guy to walk away. She could tell. He would go back if only for the sake of his two daughters. His determination to stand by his responsibilities only made her love him more. She felt a strong aching in the pit of her stomach every morning when she realized they were one day closer to him leaving. She knew she had to be strong and face the facts, but it was eating her up inside.

Danny had been pestering her to pose for him all week. Julie made a deal with him that if he would take her to the ocean, she would pose for him as long as he wanted. She'd always wanted to see the ocean and walk along a sandy beach. When Sunday came they rode the bus down to the beach. Danny brought his charcoal and sketch pad. It was a beautiful sunny day. The sky was clear and the sun was hot, but the ocean breeze kept them cool. The water was too cold for swimming, so they settled for walking barefoot in the wet sand until they found a secluded area that was hidden by some large boulders. There Julie took off her clothes and draped a towel around her body. She posed herself at Danny's direction next to a large rock. He sketched her half-naked body as she stared off at the sea.

When he'd made all the drawings he wanted, he pulled her down off the rocks and lay her down in the sand with him. He couldn't take his eyes—or his hands—off of her. Julie thought she could tell he really cared about her. She wondered if he was dreading going home as much as she was. She knew this was going to just be a temporary relationship, but she had fallen for him pretty hard. She stared back into his eyes thinking how much she would be missing them soon. They were the color of the water beside them, and now she knew she would always see his face when she looked out over the ocean. Before they left, they made love in the sand with the waves crashing just beyond the rocks. Knowing it would be their last time, they clung to each other tightly as their bodies moved together.

He didn't show up at the diner on Monday night, so she went by his motel room after work. The manager told her he had left before dawn that morning. Julie went back to her place and cried all night long. She knew he was going to leave, but it had still happened way too soon for her. It had obviously been too hard for him also, or he wouldn't have left without saying goodbye. Maybe he had loved her too? She was mad at herself for letting her feelings get that carried away. It really didn't matter how she felt about him at this point. There were no choices to be made. There was no room for her in his life. They knew they would never see each other again. All they would have is the memories.

Three weeks later Julie found out she was pregnant. Being a parent was not what she really wanted to be just yet. She had a crappy job. She lived in motel room, and she had no husband. She knew she couldn't tell Danny even if she knew how to find him. She was on her own with this one, and she had to think fast before things got more complicated. She was angry with herself for being so stupid. She was angry with Danny for being married. And she was angry for this thing inside her that could mess up her dreams of ever having a good life. She could not take care of a baby. It would only dig her deeper into the hole she was living. Sensing that she had no other options, Julie decided to have an abortion.

 She told herself it was for the best. It was a safe procedure that would be over quickly, and she could move on with her life. She told herself everything would be fine, if she could just make it past this little mistake. Petrified with the consequences of her actions but still more afraid of being a mother, Julie found herself in the waiting room of a clinic one September afternoon.

She nervously filled out the paperwork while she waited for her name to be called. Her hands were trembling. She hated what she was doing, but she was even more afraid of doing nothing. A woman holding a clipboard came out to the waiting area and escorted her back to the examination room. Sensing Julie's anxiety, the woman kept reassuring her that everything would be alright. She told her that the doctor was very gentle and had performed hundreds of these procedures on other girls just like her every day.

Julie did her best to relax and let the doctor do what he needed to do. She laid back and put her feet in the stirrups as he directed. She laid there and looked up at the ceiling and tried to think of better days. She thought about her sixth birthday party, when she was still young enough to think that life was something good. Her friends from school and her parents were gathered around the table with her as she made a wish on six glowing candles on her cake. She could almost taste that birthday cake again. She couldn't remember the last time she'd had one. Her thoughts of fluffy white icing were abruptly interrupted by the doctor saying he was finished. It was over much quicker than she expected, and before she knew it she was back out in the cold walking home.

That evening she tried her best to eat some soup she'd brought home from the deli. She was starting to cramp, and it made her feel like she was going to vomit. They told her that would be normal to experience some cramping and bleeding, so she tried to distract herself from the pain with watching television. She kept telling herself that she had done the right thing, all the while struggling with the guilt she was feeling. She could not bring a baby into her world. She could barely take care of herself, let alone another person. She didn't know how to be a mother, and she didn't want to be one.

The pain increased to the point where she could no longer concentrate on the TV anymore. She took some aspirin and started changing her clothes for bed. It felt good to get out of her jeans and slip a soft nightgown on over her head. She went to the bathroom to put a fresh maxi pad into her underwear, but when she pulled her panties down, she found she had soaked through the pad. Feeling more anxious now, she quickly changed pads and pulled her panties up so she didn't have to look at the blood. They told her there would be spotting, but this seemed too heavy for spotting. The cramping started again, and Julie began to cry out of fear and pain. Writhing around on the bathroom floor in agony, she wondered when she would ever stop making bad choices in her life and start being smart. She felt now that she had reached rock bottom. She had let herself get so low that she had talked herself into taking a human life. *Oh, Danny, why couldn't you have stayed?* Through her tears of heartache and physical torture, she begged God to forgive her for what she had done and asked Him to help her turn her life around.

3

Hannah met Paul in their junior year of college at the University of Southern Mississippi. She was an art student, and he was studying business law. Their first meeting was at the coffee shop as they each tried to collect the same fat-free caramel latte, which both of them had apparently ordered. She was immediately attracted to him—the way his dark-blonde hair fell across his forehead just above his hazel green eyes, his broad shoulders, and a smile that looked like it should be in a commercial for milk. They laughed off that first meeting and went about their day. Two hours later they tried to check out the same book from the library. "We've got to stop meeting like this," Paul said as he conceded the book to Hannah. Hannah graciously accepted the book, which she desperately needed in order to finish her paper that was due in two days, and walked out of the library. When they ended up at the same party five hours later, they decided that fate had them in its grasp, and they should at least introduce themselves.

It didn't take them long to discover that they had a great deal in common besides lattes and library books, and Paul eventually asked her out on a date. Hannah realized after their first evening together that there was something special between them. She could see herself spending her life with Paul. Apparently Paul felt the same way, because they saw each other every day after that.

In the winter of their senior year, Paul asked Hannah to marry him. Hannah accepted. She was so in love with him. He was everything she ever wanted in a boyfriend and a husband. They shared the same political views, they read the same books, and they wanted the same things from life. She knew they were going to have an amazing life together. She'd never known anyone like Paul. He was gentle and soft-spoken. He had a boyish charm about him, but he also had an air of maturity that assured her he would be a strong husband and father. Having come from a single-parent household and never knowing her father, Hannah was anxious to have a traditional family and a handful of babies running around the house.

Although they came from different backgrounds, they seemed perfectly fitted for each other. Paul came from a somewhat wealthy family in New Orleans. He was the only boy with two older sisters. He'd lived there all his life and intended to go back to work at one of the several companies downtown once he graduated. His father was well-connected and would have Paul set up for life when he returned home. Hannah had grown up in Mississippi. The only parent she ever knew was her grandmother who had lovingly encouraged her to follow her dreams of being an artist.

It seemed like there was nothing that either one didn't know about the other. He could read her like a book. He knew just how to make her laugh and when to leave her alone, because nothing could make her laugh at those times. She knew that he could get himself so focused on his studies that he would forget to eat. She also knew that a chocolate chip cookie from the coffee shop could completely shatter his concentration and get him to go for a walk in the park with her. There was only one time that Paul had been successful in completely fooling Hannah, and she would never forget it. On the one year anniversary of their first date, Paul had booked a room at a cute bed and breakfast downtown. After dinner they took a stroll down Main Street to look at the Christmas lights. The night air was very chilly, and she went immediately to take a hot shower when they returned to the room. As the hot water warmed up her cold skin, she thought about making love to Paul. He had been her first, and just like with everything else, he had been so careful and gentle with her. He seemed to always know what to do or where to touch her to make her feel satisfied. She knew tonight would be just as incredible as the first time. She stepped out of the shower and donned a terry cloth robe.

She opened the bathroom door to find Paul sitting on the side of the bed facing her. He was chewing something. She said, "What are you eating?"

"Nothing," Paul said with a guilty expression on his face.

"You are too eating something! How can you be hungry? We just ate. What are you eating?"

"A mint," he said as some chocolate dripped down the corner of his mouth.

"Where did you get it?" asked Hannah, searching the room. She was a chocoholic and Paul knew it.

"It was on my pillow," said Paul.

Hannah's eyes went immediately to the two pillows on the bed. She ran her fingers over her pillow only to be disappointed. "Where's mine?" she asked.

"I don't know. I guess they forgot to give you one," Paul said. He giggled.

Now Hannah was just a little aggravated. Why would they only leave one mint on the pillow? And even more importantly, why did Paul eat it and not give it to her? "Paul!" she said. "Did you eat mine?"

"Maybe yours fell off," Paul offered, sensing her impending anger.

Hannah bent over the bed and pulled back the blankets. Next she lifted up the pillow to see if the mint might be hiding underneath. What she found instead of a mint was a tiny diamond attached to a silver setting lying on a card that said, "Marry me."

She looked up at Paul, then back down at the ring. She screamed and started crawling across the bed to get to him. She wrapped her arms around his neck and kissed him. "Yes!" she said, and then she continued to kiss him. It was a magical night. She couldn't get over how he had pulled one over on her like that, and she could see that life with him would never be boring. He was a one-in-a-million guy and she would never let him go.

For spring break he had promised Hannah to take her back home to New Orleans to meet his folks. He also wanted her to meet his best friend and his best man, Dane. "Dane and I grew up together. We were like brothers. He was my best friend, until I met you," Paul told her. "I can't wait for you to meet him. I just know you'll love him as much as I do."

"I'm sure I will, Paul," said Hannah. "If he could be your brother, then I know I'll like him."

In March Paul and Hannah made the long-discussed trip to Louisiana. Hannah fell in love with his mom and dad almost as quickly as she had fallen in love with Paul. While they could have been such snobs to her, given their net worth, they were just as down-to-earth and kind as any two people could be. Their laid back approach to everything made her see where Paul had inherited his easy-going nature. Paul's sisters were equally nice. They were both married—one living in Baton Rouge and the other in Lake Charles. They had come in for the weekend to meet Hannah and to torment their brother by giving Hannah the inside scoop on what it was like growing up with Paul.

Paul's parents threw a huge party at their house that first night to celebrate the engagement. Their home was striking. It was an old two-story, white Victorian with a wide front porch set proudly atop a hill in the middle of the Garden District. Its graceful beauty was stately, yet charming, which matched the personalities of its inhabitants. Both floors and surrounding property were filled with friends and family that evening. Hannah was overwhelmed by the out-pouring of hospitality, warmth and genuine affection from people she had only just met.

Outside by the pool, Hannah couldn't help but notice a young man directly across it. He was tall and thin. His thick, jet black hair looked as if it had never seen a comb, but somehow didn't look out of place at all with his thick bushy eyebrows and dark brown eyes. He wore a white, long-sleeved oxford shirt that only enhanced his extremely tan skin. He wore it loosely with the tail out over a pair of faded blue jeans. He seemed to be the perfect combination of unkempt and stylish—like a GQ model. Young women were flocked all around him, laughing, talking, and pawing at him every chance they had. *I'll bet he reeks of Polo cologne,* she thought to herself. Hannah began to wonder if he was a celebrity the way he managed to draw so many people into his circle. She watched as he told story after story to these women, then let out a strong laugh. They would laugh and raise their beer bottles up in the air as if to toast his brilliance. What Hannah found puzzling was the look on his face after telling such a story. His laugh was not real. He'd let out a loud guffaw and then immediately tighten his mouth and stare off into space. She could tell that he was not in the least bit impressed with his stories or the women surrounding him. Despite all the drinking and laughing, he was extremely bored. Just then he turned his glance across the pool and looked directly into Hannah's eyes. She jumped when she realized she had been caught and quickly moved her head about searching desperately for something to focus her attention. In the midst of this embarrassing turmoil, Paul slipped his hand around her waist and saved her from more awkwardness.

"Are you having a good time?" Paul asked. His soft hazel eyes crinkled in the corners as he smiled sweetly at her. She could tell he was beginning to feel a little buzzed from the alcohol, and it made her smile to see him feeling so uncharacteristically loose.

"Yes, it's great. This party is fantastic! The house is gorgeous. Your parents are amazing, Paul. Your whole family is. I can't wait to be a part of the family!"

"You already are! They all love you." He smiled and squeezed her tightly. "C'mon, there's somebody I want you to meet," he said as he guided her by the small of her back around the pool. Much to Hannah's surprise, he walked her right up through the crowd of drunken groupies till she was face to face with the tall, dark, and very popular stranger from across the pool. She looked all around wondering where Dane was in this group of spoiled rich preppies.

"Hannah, this is Dane," said Paul as he took her head and aimed it at the man in front of her. "Dane, this is the woman I'm going to marry. This is Hannah."

Dane stared down at Hannah, but didn't say a word. His charming smile had faded into a serious straight line across his face. She could sense his immediate disappointment in her and wished so much that she could disappear at that moment, but luck wasn't with her. After what seemed like several minutes, Hannah decided to break the uncomfortable silence between them. "It's nice to finally meet you, Dane. Paul's told me so much about you."

More silence. Hannah couldn't figure out if he was so stoned he could no longer speak, or if he was more socially awkward than she had first imagined. Dane's dark brown eyes cut right through her as he moved them down her body and back up again to the top of her head. She felt herself blush at his interrogation of her. Then his eyes landed back on her eyes. He took a deep breath and said, "I always thought you would marry someone pretty." Then Dane turned to look at Paul. He smiled and walked away.

Hannah looked up at Paul with a question in her eyes. Paul looked a little puzzled also but quickly changed his expression to a carefree smile. He looked at her and said, "He's so drunk! He doesn't know what he's saying." Paul took her hand and led her inside the house so they could mingle with his parents and cousins.

The whole time Hannah kept hearing the words out of Dane's mouth. She played them over and over like a tape, trying to decipher their true meaning. *I always thought you'd marry someone pretty. Did that mean, 'I thought you'd marry someone pretty—not ugly like her,' or was he saying, 'Wow, she's really pretty, but then I always knew you'd marry someone pretty'—which was it? And how could this Neanderthal be Paul's best friend? This was the guy with whom he'd shared his childhood years? The guy who was like a brother to him? The guy who knew all his deepest thoughts and secrets?* Hannah found herself completely absorbed with curiosity and deep disappointment after what had started out to be an outstanding evening. For Paul's sake she decided to let it go for the moment and rejoin the fun. She would think about it later when there wasn't so much distraction.

The next day Paul arranged for Hannah and him to meet up with Dane for lunch in the French Quarter. On the way over, he got a call from his father to meet some important business leads at the riverfront. After much persuading, he convinced Hannah to meet Dane at the Café Maspero while he took care of this necessary business. Knowing that Paul's career and their future depended on it, she grudgingly agreed to go on her own to meet Dane. It was hard enough to get excited about spending the day with him and Paul, but the idea of having to sit at a table alone with him making small talk for several hours sounded like pure torture. She forced a smile as Paul turned to go the other way.

Jackson Square was quite lovely in the spring. The trees were in bloom, the birds were singing, and Hannah enjoyed the stroll around the park reviewing all the artists' works hanging along the iron fence and strewn on the sidewalk. At the other end of the square, musicians gathered and played, "When the Saints Come Marching In" and "Amazing Grace." Mixed in among the bugle players and accordion players were tarot card readers—stationed and ready to give you your future for ten dollars.

She was still strolling and looking at the different works of art on the fence, when one particular painting caught her eye. She stopped in front of it to study it further. It was a picture of a woman sitting on a rock next to the ocean. The beautiful aquamarine colors of the ocean and sky played so well in contrast to the woman's long flaxen hair flowing across her naked back. For some reason Hannah was quite mesmerized by this piece. As an artist, she often lost herself inside the setting of a painting or a photograph, trying to imagine what was happening in that moment to the subject. She wondered what that woman was thinking as she gazed out over the sea. *Was she waiting for the love of her life to return, or had she just finished bathing in the water and was enjoying the sun on her back?* The artist noticed her looking at it and said from his chair, "She was the love of my life."

Hannah looked over at him. She guessed him to be about fifty years old. His long gray hair which still held some remnants of brown in it from his younger days lay softly at his shoulders. His lips curled into a smile in between his bushy mustache and beard. Hannah couldn't help but think he looked like an old hippie.

"*Was*?" Hannah asked. "What happened to her?"

The man looked out at the cathedral and squinted as the wind blew his hair back. She could tell from the look on his face he was very troubled by the memory. "I don't know." He frowned. "I left her. When I realized I'd made a mistake, I went back to find her, but she was gone." He shook his head and looked back at Hannah. "It was complicated, but I waited too long. That's the thing about life. You don't always get a second chance and there are no guarantees. Love is the only thing that really matters."

Hannah watched him with pity. She felt a lump gather in her throat and she quickly glanced back at the painting. "I can see why you went back for her. She looks like she was very lovely."

"Stunning," he said as he stood up and walked over to the painting to admire its subject matter. "She was stunning." He turned and looked at Hannah. "She was the most beautiful woman I've ever seen."

"Was she happy when you painted this picture of her?" she asked.

The artist wrinkled his brow and stroked the whiskers on his chin as he contemplated her question. "I painted this from memory, months after she posed for me. The day we were on the beach I was sketching her with charcoal. Yes, I'd have to say I think she was happy that day. She was very happy. She had a need to feel free and on that particular day I think she felt it." He stared at the painting and Hannah could tell he was reliving that day all over in his mind. "Love is a very precious thing," he said. "Don't let it slip away." He smiled a big smile. Even when he was smiling Hannah couldn't help but think he looked sad the way his eyes turned down at the corners.

"I know what you mean," said Hannah. "I'm getting married this year." She smiled happily and looked down at her engagement ring.

The artist looked thoughtfully at Hannah, placed his hand on her arm and said, "That's wonderful, honey. You're very fortunate."

Hannah suddenly remembered she had to be somewhere. She glanced down at her watch and searched for the words to gently disengage from the conversation. She said, "It was nice talking with you." She smiled at him again and he smiled back, then she turned and walked away. She couldn't get his face out of her mind as she hunted for the restaurant. She felt so bad for the man to think how sad and lonely he must be without the love of his life. She couldn't imagine her life without Paul.

She spotted Dane right away inside the dark café. He was sitting at a corner table with his back up to the wall. The sunlight coming through the window on his right was like a spotlight pointing her out to him. His chin was resting on his hand and he looked like he was in deep thought as he waited. His beer was already half gone. Hannah took a deep breath and walked up to the table with a smile. She explained Paul's dilemma and looked away quickly to avoid seeing the disappointment on his face that she was sure he would display. She ordered a beer in the hopes that alcohol might give her the strength she needed to get through this painful meeting.

After a couple of muffalettas and several beers, the conversation lightened up. Hannah realized that Dane really could be funny. He had some great stories of Paul and him growing up. She found herself laughing freely, truly enjoying learning more about Paul and getting to know Dane. She was starting to see why Paul liked him so much. He was nothing like Paul, but he complemented him so well. He was dark and contemplative where Paul was light and optimistic. Despite his rough appearance and slightly clumsy social skills, Hannah could see that Dane was a thoughtful, kind-hearted friend. She saw that Dane loved Paul as much as she did. And that was enough for her to give him another chance.

They were laughing and telling stories as if they were best friends whenever Dane's phone rang. It was Paul saying he was delayed and that Dane should be sure and take Hannah to Pat O'Brien's. Hannah agreed to go, so they hit the sidewalk heading toward St. Peter Street. It was a clear, sunny day and Hannah wished she'd brought her camera to take pictures of the unique window dressings on the second floor of these old buildings. Dane gave her a short history lesson of New Orleans as they walked. "There's so much to learn here about the people and the culture. This is a very unique place. But before you do anything else, you have to try a Hurricane!" Dane laughed as he showed her into the courtyard of the famous drinking establishment. They found a small table near the fountain and sat down to warm their faces in the sun. The icy cold sweetness of the rum drink felt good as the heat from the sun began to really warm them up. After one, she was feeling very happy. Halfway through the second, Hannah was ready to say anything. She decided to take advantage of her uninhibited state to ask Dane a question that had been burning in the back of her mind since the day before.

"So, Dane, when you first met me yesterday, you said something that I didn't quite understand. You said something to Paul about thinking he would marry someone pretty. I wasn't really sure what you meant by that." She looked at him across the table. He looked so serious as she spoke. Despite her new-found bravery, she was still nervous about asking the question. She took a deep breath and said, "Do you think I'm not pretty enough for Paul to marry?"

Dane was staring at her the entire time she was talking, but now he looked away. "Hannah," he said and turned back to face her. "I was being a jerk last night. That's all you need to know." He took another sip from his glass and looked away as if he was ashamed at the memory of his behavior from last night. Hannah dropped the subject and went back to enjoying her drink. When they had both finished, Dane suggested that they see more of the Quarter before he took her back to Paul's house. They left the bar and began their walk down Bourbon Street.

Hannah had never seen such a crowd of people in a street before. The further they went down the street, the more crowded it became. They could barely move. Dane linked his hand around her arm and helped her make their way through the mass of partiers. She looked up at the balconies at half-naked women screaming down at the gawking spectators below. The pavement was wet with beer, soda, most likely urine, and she couldn't imagine what else. The smell was unbelievable. She was shocked at all that she was seeing and hearing. She felt someone tug on her arm and try to pull her into a bar, but it wasn't Dane, and she pulled away from him. She now realized that Dane no longer had a hold of her arm at all, and she looked around for his trademark oxford shirt and dark shock of hair, but she couldn't see him.

The crowd forced her to move on against her will. Now she was being spun around and wasn't sure if she was even headed in the same direction. She began to scream, "Dane! Dane!" hoping he would hear her over all the music and noise, but it was no use. The heat, the sweat, the noise and the confusion was beginning to overwhelm her and she felt herself begin to panic. She continued to scream for Dane despite the uproar, hoping that eventually he would hear her. Strangers who smelled like beer and sweat were rubbing up against her everywhere she turned. Tears came to her eyes, but Hannah pushed them back. Just then a hand grabbed hers and began pulling her. She hoped it was Dane's but couldn't tell. She let herself be led and prayed that it was in a good direction.

As the crowd thinned, she could see Dane on the other end of the strange arm. He pulled her to a cross street and then pushed her up against the side of a building. Hannah looked up at Dane's face. He looked angry and terrified all at once. He was out of breath and sweat was pouring down his face. His cotton shirt was drenched. A bead dripped from his face onto her lips. Dane's hands touched her hair and her face. It was as if he was looking her over for any missing pieces. He looked her up and down very differently from the way he had checked her out the night before. This time he was making sure she hadn't been hurt. His hands moved over her hair, brushing it out of her face. He wiped her tears from her cheeks with his thumbs. He ran his hands down to her shoulders, pulled her close to him, and held her like she was his own precious child who had wandered off. Then he pulled her away from him and held her face in his hands. He lifted her chin and he leaned down, staring into her eyes. "I thought—," he started, but he didn't finish. Instead he put his mouth on hers and kissed her hard. As shocked as she was, she didn't resist. His lips pressed firmly against hers were not forceful but full of longing—demanding more of her. She'd never felt that kind of desire and she wanted desperately to surrender to it. Her mouth opened slightly to let him know that she did not want it to end.

He stopped kissing her for a moment, but kept his lips on her face as he said, "I'm sorry. I'm so sorry!"

Hannah didn't know if he was sorry for losing her, sorry for how he'd hurt her the night before, or sorry for kissing her, knowing she was his best friend's fiancée. All she did know was that it felt good—his lips on hers, his breath in her face, his tongue filling up her mouth. She wrapped her arms around his neck and twined her fingers in his thick, dark hair. She let herself be swept up with the passion that had overtaken her and continued to kiss Paul's best friend.

Hannah woke up in the morning next to Paul. The sunlight streaming across the room told her it was already late. She rolled onto her back and looked up at the ceiling. Like a switch had been thrown, memories of yesterday came flooding back to her mind—the drinks, the crowds, the kiss. She couldn't stop thinking about the kiss. She couldn't forget the way Dane's soft, full lips melted into hers so perfectly. She couldn't stop remembering the smell of sweat and alcohol mixed with his hot breath rolling across her face. She'd never done anything like that in her life, but at that moment she wanted nothing more than to go to a hotel room and press her naked body against his. She closed her eyes and imagined his tongue inside her mouth. She felt the heat between her legs as she pictured the two of them in a hotel bed, moving together in perfect rhythm and exploding into ecstasy.

It hadn't gone that far though. The kiss ended. Dane walked her to the streetcar and gave her directions to Paul's house. Just before he put her on the car, he apologized for his behavior. She looked out the window at him standing on the sidewalk. She could see he felt terribly guilty. From the look on his face, you would have thought he'd shot his own dog. She remained quiet. She didn't know what to say, so she decided to say nothing. The streetcar gave a jerk and they were moving away. Her thoughts turned back to Paul and how distressed she must look. She had to pull herself together before she landed in the Garden District.

Paul began to yawn and stretch which pulled her out of her daydream. She looked over at him lying there bathed in soft sunlight. She loved him so much. They were perfect together. So why did she feel this deep longing to be with Dane? She could wrestle with it all day long, but in the end it really didn't matter. It was a kiss—a very passionate kiss—between two strangers who had been drinking all afternoon and got caught up in the heat of the moment. This is what she told herself in order to put it out of her mind and focus on all the good that was happening in her life with Paul.

Hannah showered, put on her makeup and curled her hair. Much to her surprise, when she stepped out of the bathroom, she found a note from Paul on the bed: *Went with Mom and Dad to see attorney. Take the garden tour! I'll see you for lunch. Love you.*

She went downstairs to make some breakfast. Before the toast could pop up, there was a knock on the door. It was Dane. He looked nervous and puzzled to see her answer the door. She explained that Paul was out with his parents. She was sure that she blushed when she realized that they were alone in the house together. To appear nonchalant she offered him a cup of coffee and—to her surprise—he accepted.

As soon as they were seated in the kitchen, Dane began apologizing for the day before. "You know, I just had too much to drink and then you were lost in the crowds…I just about went crazy looking for you. I was wondering how I was going to explain to Paul that I had lost his fiancé on Bourbon Street!" He laughed. "Then I saw you, and I was so…you know…relieved. I was so relieved and drunk and I just started kissing you. I'm sorry. And then I didn't know what to say, so I just didn't say anything." He laughed a little and then searched her eyes for a response.

Realizing that he was expecting her to speak, she jumped a bit. She had been remembering the kiss and had lost herself in the memory. She tried her best to focus on the conversation. "Yes, I completely understand. I was scared too. I was so grateful when your hand finally reached out for me and pulled me out of that mess. Really, don't think anything of it. We'll never mention it again. It's forgotten." She smiled at him, looking for his reaction to her words. She saw a look of relief on his face, but he was unable to look her in the eyes. To change the subject, she asked him what his plans were for the day. They soon discovered that neither of them had any plans, so they continued to talk over coffee until they were starving for lunch. Dane offered to take Hannah to the riverfront and she accepted, completely forgetting that Paul apparently had stood her up again and hadn't come home for lunch as he'd promised.

They had a relaxing afternoon without any anxiety. Hannah learned much more about Paul from Dane's stories of when both were younger. She was seeing Paul from a completely different perspective, which she found enlightening. She was also learning an awful lot about Dane, and she found him to be fascinating. He showed her his boat charter business and they sat on the dock looking out at the river for several hours lost in conversation. After Paul called Dane asking if he'd seen Hannah, they drove back. On the car ride home both remained quiet. She'd had a lot of fun with Dane, and it had been perfectly harmless. So why did she feel a sense of guilt? And what was with this sadness she felt as she stepped out of Dane's car in front of Paul's house? She asked Dane to come in and join them for supper, but he said he really needed to go catch up on business, since he had neglected it all day to be with her. She thanked him for the lovely day and slammed the car door. He said he was sure he'd see her again soon and then drove away.

She walked up the steps and through the front door to find Paul standing there with his arms open. "Hey! How was your day? I missed you!" She fell into his arms and he kissed her sweetly on the mouth. "Gosh, I missed you," he said. "I'm sorry I left you hanging all morning. There's just so much to work out while I'm here." He held her close and stroked the back of her hair as she laid her head on his chest. "It won't always be like this. I promise." Then they went in to have dinner with his parents. Hannah spent the entire evening thinking about her day with Dane.

Two days later Hannah found herself alone again for most of the day. It was her last full day in New Orleans, and she was tired of waiting for Paul to show her around. She dressed, grabbed a croissant for nourishment, and ran out the door to join up with the Garden District tour. Paul had mentioned it several times, and she was anxious to go. She just never thought she would be taking the tour without him. She sighed. She knew Paul was using this week to lay the groundwork for their future. His father had spent a lot of time introducing him to all the right people in the city to ensure a solid career with a reputable company. It was understandable that she had to share him. She kept telling herself that soon they would be married, and they would have their whole lives to be together.

She caught up with the tour just as they were planning to depart the bookstore. The first stop was the cemetery. Hannah marveled at the white stone tombs built above ground. It was like a little city in itself. It held such mystery, and she imagined the stories of the people buried there as she walked along the narrow paths and admired the stone and ironwork. She could have stayed in there all day pondering over the residents, but the tour was heading out to look at the homes, so she scrambled to catch up with them. Each house was more beautiful than the next in the Garden District, and she couldn't wait to get started picking out her favorite. She could see herself living here and raising their children in one of these gorgeous homes with the big yards and iron fences.

The group crossed the street and made its way to the first of many beautiful mansions, when she heard her name being called from a distance. Hannah turned her head around and stood on her tiptoes to gaze above the tourists to see who was calling out for her. She was filled with hope that Paul had decided to join her after all. She stopped in her tracks and let the people go by so she could see more clearly. "Hannah!" he called. He was getting closer. The last of the tour group walked around her and there on the corner was Dane. She flushed with excitement at the sight of him.

"Hannah, I thought that was you," Dane said as he came up to meet her. "I was going to get a bite to eat and there you were in this crowd of tourists!" He twisted his brow together displaying his bewilderment that she was a part of a tour. She tried desperately to not notice how adorable it made him look. Dane invited her to get some lunch and promised to take her on a private tour of the district afterwards. She accepted. She wasn't sure if it was hunger or Dane that was making her feel a bit light-headed, but she thought a meal might do her some good. They walked back to the little café on the corner to have some sandwiches and iced tea. The weather was pleasant as usual so they sat outside and fed their crumbs to the birds. Dane seemed to be almost chipper today, so unlike when Hannah first met him. She was watching him talk about his mother and father.

"Didn't you say you were from Jackson?" Dane asked.

"Yes I am," said Hannah.

"My sister lives up there with her husband and kids. I went to visit her last year and went to this awesome estate auction…brought back some great things. It's a nice place," he said.

"Yes it is," said Hannah. But she wasn't really concentrating on what he was saying. She was more interested in watching his mouth as he spoke. His teeth were bright white against his tan skin and would have given him the perfect smile, if it weren't for the fact that they were just the slightest bit crooked in front. When he laughed, he laughed fully and genuinely—not like the other night when he was telling jokes to all those fawning girls. He trusted her enough to be *real* with her and that made her feel good.

After lunch Dane took Hannah for a walk through the beautiful neighborhoods she'd been dying to see. Each house was more exquisite than the last. While the all-brick stately mansions spoke of class and elegance, Hannah was more drawn to the Victorian style houses with their wraparound porches and brightly colored gingerbread trim. They were walking and talking, discussing art and history, when Dane stopped in front of one of the smaller Victorian homes. The color was unusual. It was a pale pinkish-orange. The trim was painted light and dark green and the door was mahogany. The yard—filled with rose bushes of every color—was surrounded by a dark green painted decorative cast iron fence. It looked like something out of a storybook to Hannah.

"Why did you stop here?" she asked.

"This is my favorite house in the district. I wanted to show it to you." He took her by the hand, started through the gate, and headed toward the backyard. "Let's check it out. I've heard it's haunted. I don't think anyone is home, but I know where they leave a key. C'mon!"

"Dane!" she squealed. "We can't just break into someone's house!"

"It's okay. I know the owners. They won't mind. Come on!" he said as he dragged her up the back steps to the door. He pulled a key out from under the rug and let them both inside. Immediately they were in the kitchen. It appeared to have been recently updated with new appliances. Dane watched as Hannah looked all around the room at the beautiful wood molding at the top and bottom of the walls and the oak hardwood floor. A charming antique table and chairs sat in the center of the room. He could tell by her expression that she was pleased with what she saw.

"It looks like a perfect place to have a tea party," Hannah said as her eyes continued to roam. Then coming to her senses, she said, "This is quite lovely, but, Dane, we should go." She turned toward the door and took a step.

"It's okay, Hannah," he said. He grabbed her hand just as she tried to walk out the door. He pulled her back toward him. "This is my house," he said.

Hannah's eyes became like round saucers. "What? It's yours?"

He started laughing at her surprise, which aggravated her. She reached up to fake a slap at him. "You're mean! You tricked me!"

Dane reached up to grab her hand before it had a chance to reach his cheek. Their fingers intertwined as he pulled her hand down to her side. Sensing the force growing between them, he cleared his throat, let go of her hand, and said, "Let me show you the rest of it."

With that she took off to study the rest of the house. Dane followed her into the living room that was still in need of furniture, and then they both proceeded up the steep wooden staircase. "I just bought the place, so it still needs a lot of furniture and decorating. Maybe after you and Paul move down here you can help me," he said in a hopeful-sounding, question-like voice. Hannah didn't reply. She continued to open every door and peek into every room, commenting on everything she saw that she liked and how she would change what wasn't up to her standards. Dane followed her around like a well-trained pup, smiling. He was delighted with her reaction.

He stood in front of the last door at the hall and said, "So what do you think?"

Hannah looked at him with a questioning expression. "What's in this room?" she asked.

"It's just my room," he said. "Tell me what you think of the house."

"Well, I haven't seen the whole house yet," she said as she tried to reach past him and grab the doorknob.

Dane stood aside so she could enter the room. He was slightly nervous as he spoke. "I put this room together myself."

Hannah walked into the room and gasped. It was lovely. There was no denying it. She was terribly impressed with the mahogany bed with large posts on the headboard and footboard, the matching dresser, chest and side tables. The periwinkle blue walls gave the room a cool and restful feel. She walked over to the fireplace and ran her fingers over the white marble mantle.

"This is what I bought in the estate auction up in Jackson," Dane said proudly as he leaned against the large footboard and rubbed his hand over the rich dark wood of the bed post. "I got a great deal on it. What do you think?"

"I love it, Dane. I wouldn't change a thing." Hannah stopped roaming and looked directly into his eyes, to make sure he knew she was sincere. "It's a beautiful room."

"I'm glad you like it." He had been avoiding eye contact but now was forced to keep his gaze on hers. He blushed.

There was an intense energy between them. She could not deny it. She had stayed too long fixated on him, and now she was struggling with two possible actions. She could run out the door or rush into his arms. She felt herself begin to tremble as her body struggled with confusing messages from her head and her heart. Just then the clock on the mantle chimed four times. Hannah tried to take a breath, but it was shallow. It suddenly felt very warm in the room and her palms were sweating. "It's four o'clock. I need to get back," she said rather weakly. She turned and walked toward the door. As she reached the doorway, she felt his hands gently rest on her arms. She felt his breath on the back of her head, and she felt her willpower leave the room without her.

She could tell that he was just as afraid as she was. He just stood there behind her, very softly running his fingers down her light brown hair. She could tell he was breathing in her scent and wrestling with his own mind and heart about what should happen next. He leaned his forehead on the back of her head. She could feel his frustration. Somehow knowing this was just as difficult for him, made it that much more easy for her to allow it to happen. She turned very slowly in his arms and raised her head for him to kiss her. She knew she should fight it, but she had to let him have her. She had to know what it felt like to be his.

4

Julie met Michael in 1980. She moved to Daytona two years earlier and found a job as a receptionist in a medical office. She had recently been promoted to Office Manager. Michael was a new medical supplies sales rep who was trying desperately to charm his way into seeing her boss—the doctor. He was not as much charming as he was downhearted. She took pity on him and made an appointment for him to deliver his sales pitch to the doctor the following Wednesday.

On Wednesday—after meeting with her boss—he asked her out for dinner. Michael was the sweetest man Julie had ever met. He wasn't the kind of guy that Julie was usually attracted to, with his short cut, sandy-blonde hair, dark-framed glasses, and stocky build, but he was kind, thoughtful, and seemed to be genuinely interested in her. Of course, there were many things Julie never told him about her. As much as she wanted to believe he could love her unconditionally, she was afraid that too much information could destroy what they had together. She wasn't sure if Michael could understand her earlier childhood situation and why she had made the choices she had. He had grown up very sheltered with a strong family background. They were not wealthy, but his father had done well in real estate, so

Michael had never wanted for anything. Julie saw her chance to be part of a real family, and she wasn't about to let anything spoil it. After three months of dating, he asked her to marry him. They had a small ceremony a year later in Michael's church surrounded by his friends and family. Julie told them that she had no family, and in her mind it was the truth.

She devoted herself to her new husband. It was a whole new world for her. She loved her life, and she loved Michael. He was succeeding in sales, and they were able to purchase a beautiful house that exceeded Julie's wildest dreams. They tried to start a family but failed. Michael suggested that they go for testing, but Julie didn't want to pursue it for fear that she would have to explain her past experiences. She was disappointed of course, but never let it show too much to him. He didn't seem to mind the lack of children. His career was soaring and he was on the road nearly every week. It meant that there were some lonely times along the way for her, but she was too grateful for the life she had to ever complain. Although he was gone quite often with work, Michael was devoted to her, and that was all she ever really wanted. Julie didn't need to work anymore, but she kept her job just to keep herself occupied while Michael was on the road. It gave her a sense of purpose. She'd become well respected at work with her knack for organization and management skills. For the first time in her life, Julie felt loved, admired, and appreciated.

Things were going very well for them, and Julie could see their future would be bright and anything but boring. She had a house near the ocean, which was something she'd always wanted. She spent a lot of time out there on the beach watching the waves crashing. Memories of those days with Danny would creep in while she walked barefoot along the sand, but she would quickly shut them out of her mind. They had been good times, but nothing she could pin her future on. She was certain she'd found everything she wanted with Michael. She was very content to let their lives go on exactly as they were for many years. Then one evening she was asked to stay late at the office to help with some computer glitch which had affected their billing. She came home at six thirty to find Michael in a panic.

"Where have you been?" he asked. His eyes looked desperate and wild. They'd been married for three years and she'd never seen him so distraught.

"I had to work late. I left a message for you on the machine, so you wouldn't worry. Didn't you check?" she asked innocently.

Michael didn't even glance at the machine. Instead, he fumed back at her, "Are you seeing somebody?"

Julie was speechless, but his persistence forced her to find something to say. "Michael! Of course not!" she pleaded. "I told you I had to work late. I'm so sorry I worried you." She began to take out food from the refrigerator to prepare dinner, hoping he would cool off as she did so. He was quiet for a while as she pulled out some pans from the cabinet, and she hoped that would be the end of the conversation. Unfortunately it was not.

He said, "You're just going to have to quit your job. We don't need the money. I'd feel better if I knew you were at home. Then this will never happen again."

Julie laughed lightly. "Oh sure, I'll just stay at home and twiddle my thumbs all day," she said jokingly as she peeled some carrots over the sink. She was still amazed at his behavior.

Just then she felt him grab her by the shoulders and push her up against the wall. Her head made a loud thump as it hit the plaster. Now she was terrified. She couldn't believe that this was happening, and she trembled as he squeezed her arms tightly until they hurt.

"I'm dead serious, Julie. You're putting in your notice tomorrow." She could feel his hot breath on her face. "You're my wife and I provide a good life for you. There's no reason for you to be working. I need you here taking care of our home."

"Okay, Michael," she said very quietly. "If that's what you want, I'll tell them tomorrow." Tears were welling up in her eyes, and she was trying very hard to keep them from falling. She didn't want to let him see how afraid she was of him at that moment.

Michael relaxed his grip on her and calm returned to his face. He stroked her hair with his fingers and said, "Alright then. It's settled." He moved aside so she could get back to preparing dinner.

Michael never became that angry with her ever again, but Julie still kept the memory of that night in the back of her mind. It changed everything for her. It killed the respect she had for him. It destroyed the whole nature of their relationship. She no longer felt like Michael's partner. She didn't know if she could ever love him again. Still, she had made a commitment to this marriage, and she had every intention of honoring it. She had to find a way to make it work between them. After all, he had given her so much.

The next few years were very different for her. She missed her job and her friends. Michael suggested that they join the country club, so she could meet some new friends, but she didn't think she was the country club type. Michael paid the dues for membership, but she never went. Instead she would go shopping and spend her summers at the beach. She loved to feel that ocean breeze in her face and taste the saltiness on her lips. She would often stand at the water's edge and imagine taking off like a bird straight into the wind. She longed to feel that free again, like she had when she first came to Florida.

Michael was making more money than ever, but it meant he was gone even more as his territory grew. Julie was alone from Monday until Friday afternoon, when he returned. She didn't really mind his absence. At least when he was gone she was free to move about as she pleased. The years rolled by despite her boredom. They moved into a larger house that they didn't need at the urging of Michael, who felt the need to look as successful as he thought he was. Every year they took an extravagant trip for their anniversary. Julie saw places she never thought she would see, like Europe and the Caribbean. But even for all the beautiful places they went, her loneliness continued. No matter how far away they traveled, she still felt caged. There was no escape.

For their tenth wedding anniversary, Michael announced that he was adding a pool and enclosing it with a screened room for her. "You spend so much time at the beach. Now you won't have to. You'll have the water right outside your bedroom door," he said proudly. It was a wonderful present, and Julie was grateful to be getting it, but it didn't hold the thrill that his gifts once held for her. Once again, another door was being closed and a wall put up to keep her bounded. She tried her best to look pleased as Michael's eyes searched for her approval of his idea.

Once they had a finalized plan, Michael turned the project over to Julie to deal with on her own. He didn't have the time to devote to it, given his job. Julie was to work directly with Steve, the project manager that he had hired to do the work. Steve promised to have the final drawings to her the following week so they could get started on construction.

On Thursday Steve called and asked Julie if he could stop by with the plans. She agreed and he came by at twelve-thirty. He handed her the rolled up set of drawings and told her how pleased he was with how they had turned out. He was extremely excited to get started. Steve glanced down at his watch and said, "Gosh, I didn't realize what time it was. I hope I didn't interrupt your lunch." Julie said that he hadn't. She had eaten a late breakfast and had no intention of having lunch that day. Steve said, "That's too bad. I was hoping you could buy me lunch somewhere." He laughed.

"Really?" Julie asked somewhat shocked by his words. Playfully she added, "I would think you should be taking me to lunch, since you're the one who wants the work!" She smiled at him.

"I was hoping you'd say that," said Steve. "I'd love to take you to lunch. How about tomorrow?"

Julie was taken completely off guard by his comment and had no words. She just stood there looking at him, smiling and hoping her eyes didn't reveal her naiveté. She looked into his soft blue eyes and saw a look that she hadn't seen in a very long time. She could feel herself blushing. Julie looked around the room as if she thought someone might be watching them and said quietly, "I don't think that would be a good idea, but thank you for the invitation."

Steve moved in a little closer. "Are you sure? I'd really like to take you to lunch. We could discuss the drawings and the schedule for the project. If you want to have this done before summer's over, we'll have to get started soon."

Now Julie felt foolish. She was reading way too much into this. After all, this guy had to be at least ten years younger than she was. She smiled back at him reassured that this was purely a business invitation. "Of course," she said. "That's a great idea. Just tell me where to be, and I can meet you at noon."

"Sounds good," said Steve. "How 'bout I pick you up at your house at noon?"

Julie agreed with some hesitation. He left before she could change her mind. Although she told herself it was completely innocent, she still felt a little giddy at the thought of going out with this terribly handsome young man.

He picked her up the next day in his truck. She was impressed when he opened the door for her, but she was embarrassed of the view he had of her as she desperately climbed up into the seat. When he got in on his side, she looked over at him. He looked wonderful, she thought. He was wearing a light blue button-down shirt and dark jeans. His light brown hair was cut short and he was clean shaven. Julie sniffed the air. He smelled nice too. She doubted that he had agonized over what he wore today as much as she had. She'd spent the entire morning trying on outfits. One made her look too old. One made her look like she was trying to look too young. She eventually settled on a sundress, light sweater, and sandals. She pulled her long straight hair back in a ponytail.

As they drove to the restaurant, she kept thinking about Michael and what he would do if he found out that she'd had lunch with this man who was a virtual stranger. He was out of town as usual. There was probably no reason to think he would find out. Still she was uneasy about the whole thing. She looked up into the mirror on the truck's visor. She saw the crow's feet around her eyes and quickly put on her sunglasses. *What was she doing with this guy?* She glanced at Steve out of the corner of her eye to see if he was paying any attention to her nervous behavior. He just looked straight ahead. Then, without taking his eyes off the road, he said, "You look great by the way." Julie smiled and thanked him.

They had lunch at an outdoor sidewalk café. It was cloudy, but still very warm and humid. They did just as he said they would and discussed the details of the pool project. There were also personal comments added in as well. By the end of the two-hour lunch she knew about his professional background, his goals, where he was born, that he was not married, and his favorite food was a cheeseburger. Julie told him little about herself. There wasn't much to tell. The last ten years of her life were pretty much a blank slate.

After lunch, they strolled down the boardwalk. Julie couldn't remember when she'd enjoyed an afternoon with anyone, let alone a man who seemed to be possibly interested in her. When they arrived back in her driveway, they were engaged in carefree conversation. Julie was unaware that her guard had been dropped. She no longer felt nervous and uncomfortable. They were just two people having a wonderful afternoon.

"Thanks for lunch Steve. I had a great time," she said with her hand on the door handle.

Steve leaned over and put his hand on her left hand and said, "I had a nice time too, Julie." She wasn't sure if he was planning on kissing her at that point or not. She smiled and pulled her hand away gently so as not to suggest that she was reading anything into his actions. She got out of the truck and walked inside. She walked slowly and carefully up the walk just in case he was watching her. She wanted to leave him with a good impression of her.

Michael came home on Friday, and they spent a relaxing weekend together. He told her all about his trip, and he asked about her week. She neglected to tell him about her lunch with Steve, but she thought of little else all weekend. She began to wonder what would have happened if she had stayed in his truck a little longer. Would he have leaned over and kissed her? Different possible outcomes of the afternoon kept running through her mind, and she found it difficult to even engage in conversation with Michael. In fact she was feeling a bit irritated that he was even around and hopeful that Monday would come quickly, so he would go back to work.

Steve called her Monday afternoon to let her know they would be starting the project the next week. They engaged in chit-chat for a short while, and then he said, "I've been thinking about you." After a hesitation and some careful deliberation, Julie admitted that she had been thinking about him also. She felt a warm rush come over her as she said those words to him. She couldn't believe she was feeling this way nor having this kind of conversation with another man. She felt guilty for even participating, but she couldn't find the strength to hang up on him.

Steve asked if they could meet again. "Listen," he said. "I'm attracted to you, and you're attracted to me. I know you're married, but sometimes you need to take a little break from reality. It's like therapy. It's a chance to recharge. You're a beautiful, sexy woman, and you need to be treated as such. I can do that for you."

She got quiet as she mulled over what he had just said. Her heart was pounding. Deep down inside she was thrilled that a younger man who was outrageously sexy could find her attractive at her age. Caught up in the moment, she told him she would think about it.

"I'm going to call you on Thursday, and I'm going to ask you to meet me at a motel. You think about it. I want you, Julie. I think we could be amazing together." Then he hung up the phone, leaving her hanging on the other end with her mouth open and speechless. Her mind was whirling with excitement, as if she was a teenager again. She ran to the bathroom mirror to study her reflection. *I am still beautiful and desirable,* she thought to herself and she smiled at the woman staring back at her in approval. Then she thought about Michael. She pictured that look that he had in his eyes the night he told her she would have to quit her job. The enthusiasm began to drain out of her as she realized she was bound to this man. If he ever found out about Steve, he would probably kill them both. It was too much to risk.

On Thursday morning the phone rang. She was just about to step into the shower and wondered if she should instead of answering. She knew it would be him and dreaded the conversation, but she picked it up anyway and nervously said "Hello."

"Hey," was his greeting. "Whatcha doin'?"

"Just reading a book," she lied. "What are you doing?"

"On my way to the motel. You gonna meet me there?"

She struggled for a deep breath and painfully answered, "No. I can't do it." She trembled as she waited for his reaction.

After a brief silence, he said, "You can't?" Then there was a longer silence.

"I'm sorry," she said. "I'm sorry. I just can't do this."

More silence. She wondered if he had hung up on her. Then he said, "Hey, that's okay…I guess. I mean… it's no big deal…I guess."

She knew it was a big deal from the tone of his voice. Another moment of silence ensued.

"Well, I'll let you go, then," he said.

"Okay," she said, "I'll talk to you later." But she was pretty sure there would not be a "later." She stepped into the shower and sobbed as the water fell upon her face. She didn't know why she was crying. She'd done the right thing—for once. *Move on,* she told herself, *just move on.*

The following week Steve and his crew showed up to begin work on the addition. He was pleasant to her but didn't mention anything about their last conversation. Julie sat in her living room watching him work in her backyard. She couldn't help thinking how handsome he was. She liked watching him when he didn't know she was. He would bark out orders to the crew, and it excited her to see him being so confidently in command. Sometimes he would take off his shirt to do some heavy work by hand, and she would run her eyes over every muscle on his chest and on his arms. That was her favorite time of day.

She was becoming obsessed with him, and she didn't know how to stop. She didn't want to stop. She saw his face in her mind all the time. She remembered his hand on hers as they said goodbye after lunch. She started fantasizing about what could have happened if she hadn't gotten out of the truck so quickly that afternoon. She pictured him leaning over and kissing her passionately. She thought about him moving his hands under her dress and making her come with his fingers while they sat in her driveway. Nearly every morning when she was showering, she would imagine him walking into her bathroom and stepping into the shower with her. His hands would grab her around the waist as she felt his muscular arms. She could see him running his hands along her soapy body, over her breasts before turning her around and pushing her up against the wall to take her from behind.

Julie was beginning to get used to this new life she had, which was filled with sexual fantasy. It kept her mind occupied while she performed menial tasks around the house, and she was safe from ever being caught. One day she was standing at the kitchen sink washing dishes. She was staring out the window at the construction site, and her thoughts had turned to her favorite shower scene. She imagined the water cascading over their bodies while their tongues explored each other's mouths. Then she heard a voice.

"Julie? I need your opinion…" Steve's voice was right behind her and startled her out of her daydream. She turned quickly around to see him standing in her kitchen. He glanced down at her hands and said, "Hey, are you alright? You're bleeding!"

Julie looked down to see her hands covered in bloody, soapy water. She gasped and turned back toward the sink to rinse them off. She must have cut her hand on a knife but hadn't even noticed with her thoughts occupied elsewhere. Steve came over to the sink, grabbed her hands, and held them under cold running water. Julie started to cry.

"Hey, I don't think it's bad. It just looks bad from all the soap, see?" He looked at her teary face. "What's wrong?" he asked, as he grabbed a dish towel and wound it around her hand.

Julie struggled for words. Caught in the middle of a sexual fantasy only to be awakened by the man she desired so much had left her overwhelmed. "Steve," she started. "Steve, I…I…" but she couldn't say it. She couldn't tell him that she wanted him. She couldn't explain that the fantasy of making love to him had completely taken over her daily life and was making it impossible for her to function as a normal person anymore. He stood there looking into her eyes, holding her hands. She felt helpless and confused. It was hard to be this close to him and not want to kiss him. She closed her eyes and tried to make the words come, but instead she felt his mouth meet hers.

He let go of her hands and slipped his arms around her waist. Their lips locked tightly together in long passionate kisses. His hands fondled her breasts then moved down to her butt. She ran her hands across his muscular shoulders before she slid them up under his t-shirt to feel his well-defined chest. All she wanted was to be naked right now. Taking her sighs as a cue, Steve pulled her shorts down around her feet. He lifted her up onto the counter and unfastened his jeans. He pulled her back towards him, so he could get inside her. She pulled her feet up onto the counter, so she could get better traction and he could get deeper. He moved in and out of her while she moaned with unbelievable delight. Steve pulled her back towards him and said, "Let's find a bed." Julie wrapped her legs around him as he carried her to the bedroom, still inside her the whole way. They fell onto the bed without breaking their connection and continued thrusting wildly until they both climaxed in an explosion of screams.

Julie sat at her dressing table after Steve went home. She looked at her face in the mirror. Her skin was glowing, and she could no longer see those crow's feet around her eyes. She'd forgotten just how incredible passionate sex could be. She felt so alive. The way he wanted her made her feel young and sexy again.

She went back over every detail of the afternoon's events in her mind. He'd given her multiple orgasms before he finished. They lay next to each other on the bed, gasping for air and laughing at their crazy spontaneous behavior. Steve told her how amazing she was, and he wanted to do it again soon. Then he dressed and left.

As wonderful as it was, Julie speculated whether she should really see him again. She thought about Michael and decided that this should be the one and only time. It wasn't that she felt so much guilty for cheating on Michael as she was afraid that he would hurt her if he ever found out. Then she thought about Steve and how difficult it would be for her to deny him if he came onto her again. Maybe he was lying when he said he wanted to do it again. Maybe there would never be another opportunity. A young man like that probably just enjoys the initial conquests and then moves onto someone else. She decided she was thinking too much, and she would just have to see what happened next. There was no way to predict the future.

She heard Michael come in just then. She closed her eyes and took a deep breath. It was time to return to reality. She looked at her reflection and put on her fake smile of a loving wife.

5

Hannah woke up in her apartment back in Mississippi. She lay there and thought about that last afternoon with Dane. After he closed the bedroom door, he took her by the shoulders and turned her around to face him. His hot mouth felt amazing against hers. Their lips melted together as their tongues wildly tangled. Feeling his tongue penetrating her made her body yearn for the rest of him. All she wanted to do at that moment was surrender—to let him do whatever he wanted to her body.

He pulled at her blouse buttons to quickly undress her, while she strained to get his polo shirt from around his head. Her hands explored his chest and brawny arms as he squeezed her breasts. He picked her up and carried her to his bed. There he laid her down and crawled up on top of her. He bent down to kiss her again and then stopped. Hannah put her hands up to his face and looked at him with a question in her eyes. "Hannah, I can't do this," he said. He rolled over onto his back and lay there beside her with his arm over his eyes, as if he could block out everything that was happening if he didn't look at it. They both lay on their backs looking up at the ceiling and out of breath. Hannah looked over at him after a few moments. He wouldn't even look at her. Feeling frustrated and guilty, she dressed and left him in his room without saying a word. She walked back to Paul's house in complete shame.

It had been the most tumultuous four days of Hannah's life— their first kiss on that hot afternoon, the glances secretly exchanged when they thought no one was watching them, the long talks they had about what they both wanted from life, and then almost making love to him—these were the memories she could not easily forget. No matter how hard she tried, she could not drive his face, his kisses, his story and her feelings for him out of her thoughts. Even now, as she lay in her own bed, she realized she was touching herself while remembering that afternoon with him.

Time would heal the guilt, the shame and the confusion, she told herself. Time and distance would make everything right again. After all, Dane had not spoken another word to her after that day. He never tried to get in touch with her. Although it hurt her, she knew it was the right thing to do. She was glad that at least one of them had some strength.

In a very short period of time, she had come to know just about everything about Dane. She knew he had started a boat charter business after high school. College had not been his thing, so he asked his parents to invest in his business rather than his education. He started out with two boats and in four years it had grown to six boats. He'd added some guided tours, and business was booming for him. He paid his parents back and put a down payment on a house that he'd always wanted. He'd never sought the corporate ladder. He didn't see any reason to work for someone else's dream when he could build his own. She admired his ambition and determination to take charge of his life and do what he loved. But she had to stop thinking about him.

Hannah was an art major and planned to make photography her profession. She had some fantastic photos from the French Quarter, which she had taken when she and Dane had spent the afternoon strolling through the city. When she started developing the photos back at school, she ran across one of Dane in front of his business. She had decided to frame it and send it to him, but she hadn't quite gotten around to it yet, so it was lying on her desk where she could continually see it. Today she was committed to sending it off to him. She needed to get rid of him from her life. That meant all photos were to be removed and all memories must be tucked away—never to be brought out again. She sighed and rolled over in her bed. It was time to put those memories away and move on with reality. She was getting married soon!

The next two months passed very quickly and right after graduation, Hannah and Paul went to New Orleans to make wedding plans and find a house. The wedding would be held at Paul's parents' home in late October. They all agreed that the weather would be best for an outdoor celebration and the gardens should all look spectacular as the cooler temperatures came in. Although there would be a large guest list with Paul's family, friends and business associates, the wedding party would be small. Paul, of course, had chosen Dane to be his best man. Hannah's only family was her grandmother. She couldn't think of anyone she wanted more standing beside her on her wedding day than her wonderful Nana, and so she would be her maid of honor. There really wasn't much to plan with Paul's mother in charge of everything. All Hannah really had to do was choose her flowers. She and Nana had bought her wedding dress back home. It was a new dress but had a vintage 1920's look to it. Hannah loved the simple lines of the white satin that evoked a classic, feminine look. It was the most beautiful dress she had ever seen. The minute she walked into the dress shop, her eyes were drawn to it. She knew it was the gown she had to have. The veil was the jewel in the crown. It was a long train of fine, transparent, white silk that trailed down to her feet. It was held to her head by a white lace cap encrusted with pearls. She stared at herself dressed in the gown and veil standing in front of the bridal shop mirror. She felt like a princess who had found her happy ending. Her grandmother agreed that it was perfect for her as she stood drying her happy tears with a tissue. Everything was falling into place perfectly.

The greatest challenge was to find a house. At one time Hannah had been strongly in favor of living in the Garden District. But as they shopped available houses, nothing seemed to truly win her favor. Perhaps it was because there were already too many distractions. Everywhere she looked was a memory of Dane. He was standing on the corner by the cemetery, in the bookstore café at the corner table, or sitting on a park bench reading a line from his favorite book to her. Perhaps it was that no other house in the area held an interest to her since she'd already seen the one house that she wanted to make her own. She knew all this would be too much for her to start clean with

Paul. She convinced him it would be better to live closer to the business district. In fact, after being overwhelmed by so many choices in the sweltering June heat, she talked him into renting an apartment. It would be wiser to wait until they were more settled before making such an important decision. Paul smiled at Hannah after she had argued her point to rent for their first six months, admiring her practicality.

She loved how Paul let her be herself with him. No one other than her Nana had ever loved her so unconditionally. No one else had been so supportive. She was thankful for this man who would give her a lifetime of happiness. She was relieved also to realize that she had made the right choice to be with him and let go of a mysterious attraction, a momentary lapse in judgment, and a future of uncertainty.

The summer rushed by while Hannah looked for a job. She was offered a position with the Chamber of Commerce and took it, excited to be involved in creating more interest in the development of this great city that would be her new home. She also had an opportunity to use some of her creativity with the chamber's website and printed materials. Paul was consumed with his new profession, which left them apart often. Hannah used the time she had on her own to explore and take photographs. And just as they were getting used to the summer heat, it was over.

The night before their wedding, Paul went to stay with his parents, so Hannah could have the apartment to herself in the morning for getting ready. She was too anxious to sit in an empty apartment all night, so she'd grabbed a quick sandwich, looked through some of the stores on Canal Street and then strolled over to the Quarter. She wandered in and out of shops just like a tourist, smelling hand-made soaps and sampling freshly made pralines. She remembered her first time walking through Jackson Square when she was trying to find Dane and dreading their lunch together. It all seemed pretty funny to her now. Who would have thought that the day would end as it had? She smiled when she thought about it.

The sun was going down and the gaslights were glowing around Jackson Square. The artists were taking down their paintings and packing them away for another night. She wondered what became of that man with the picture of the woman on the beach. She looked for him in the place where she had seen him last March, but he wasn't there. She struggled to remember what he had said that day back in the spring. Something about knowing when it was right and not getting too many second chances? Suddenly a strange feeling of uneasiness ran over Hannah, but she brushed it off as last minute wedding jitters. It was getting dark, so she started on her way home.

Out of the shadows in Pirate's Alley a woman's voice said, "You need some help, girl?" Hannah stopped and looked into the dark space between the shops to seek out the person attached to the question. In the glow of the gas lights emerged the figure of a tiny Creole woman. "Come wit me, girl," the woman said. "Come, sit down and I tell you tings."

Normally Hannah would have just ignored the woman, but she was in no hurry this evening. She was in a romantic mood and decided to play along. She slipped behind a beaded curtain that was nearly impossible to see in the darkness. Behind the curtain the woman sat at a small table with only a tiny oil lamp for light. Hannah sat down opposite the woman.

"You need my help, girl," she said. The woman took Hannah's soft, pale hands in her dark, leathery-skinned fingers. "Your heart is torn, girl. Why your heart torn like dat?"

Hannah looked at the woman in confusion but she could feel the blood rush to her cheeks. She reminded herself that this was all a show. The woman couldn't possibly know anything about these last few months of her life. "What do you mean?" asked Hannah. She giggled nervously as she asked, "What do you see?"

The old woman continued as she studied Hannah's palms, rubbing her aged fingers across them. "You think you confused. You mind tell you that you love two men, but you heart only belong to one." The old woman looked into Hannah's eyes. "You gotta let go of your mind, girl. You gotta let your heart lead you."

"No," said Hannah abruptly. She'd had enough at playing the game. "I'm getting married tomorrow. My heart is not torn and I'm not confused. I know exactly what I'm doing!" She paused and thought about what she had just said, and then she continued, "What I mean is that I *am* following my heart. It has led me to the love of my life and I'm going to marry him tomorrow." She heard the words coming out of her mouth, but why did it sound like she was trying to convince herself of something? It was getting extremely warm in that cramped little space and Hannah could feel the heat in her face and her palms sweating.

"Da heart know what it wants," said the old woman. "But da mind get in da way. Da heart tell you what it wants. If ya don't listen to what da heart say, den da universe gonna tell ya with signs. You gotta watch for da signs. Stop lis'n' to ya brain. Brain is for aritmetic." She smiled at Hannah to reveal just a few dark crooked teeth within the dark cavern of her mouth. She took Hannah's left hand and ran her fingers around her diamond engagement ring. She held up the ring to Hannah's face. "Most people tink dat love is a diamond. It shiny and make you feel good." She shook her head disapprovingly and continued, "But love is a pearl. It don't reflect the light. It glow from within."

Hannah sat there staring at the woman trying to make sense of what she was saying. The woman let go of Hannah's hands and leaned back in her chair. She took out a tiny pipe and put it in her mouth. She smiled contentedly and continued to stare back into Hannah's eyes. "Da man who hold ya heart...he da one that hold da pearl." Then she started laughing in a tiny "teehee" fashion. Hannah rose from her chair, frightened and confused by all that had been said. She handed the woman a twenty dollar bill and walked away.

More puzzled than ever she walked back to her apartment. The woman's words rolled over and over in her mind. *Da heart know what it wants.* She laughed at herself for taking this old woman's words so seriously. Of course she knew what her heart wanted. It wanted Paul. She'd known it since their first date. They were destined to be together. If the universe was playing games with her it was by sending Dane in to confuse her. But she had seen the signs and they all pointed to Paul. Tomorrow was the beginning of the rest of their lives together. Tomorrow would be the happiest day of her life. So why now did she just feel like crying? Some flashes of lightning in the distance distracted her thoughts and she quickened her steps back to the apartment to avoid getting caught in a downpour.

The thunder boomed and the rain poured in torrents that night. Hannah stared out the window of her apartment watching the storm rage outside. She prayed that it would all be over long before she walked down the aisle in the morning. She missed Paul. She felt like she had barely seen him all summer. Things had changed so much since they were at school. He was climbing the ladder of success, and she was trying to find her niche in the art world. There was no time for a honeymoon at the moment. They had decided to go to Mexico in the early spring instead, but now she wished that they were boarding a plane tomorrow and heading away from this place. She felt a sudden urge to get away from it all.

Hannah took a long hot bath with lavender salts to relax her. She wanted to sleep well tonight so she would look her best tomorrow. It had been a warm day and it felt good to get the dirt from the Quarter off of her. After her bath, she wrapped up in a long, white terrycloth robe and brushed her hair before settling on the couch to paint her nails. It was ten o'clock, and she knew she had to wind down soon so she could get that much-needed beauty sleep. She poured herself a glass of chardonnay and flipped on the TV to see what mindless show she could watch to help settle her brains for the night. Another bolt of lightning struck so near that it made her jump as it lit up the entire sky. The electricity went out and she was now stuck there in the dark.

Slightly annoyed by the inconvenience, she went stumbling to the kitchen for matches and candles. As she made her way, the lightning and thunder continued to crash around her. In between stubbing her naked toes on the furniture, the thunder would clap and send her jumping up in a fright. She laughed as she thought how silly she looked just then—cursing and jumping every few minutes. The wine was obviously working its magic on her, but then the thought of seriously falling in this room made her sober up quickly. The last thing she wanted to be was a black and blue bride tomorrow. She decided to treat the trip back to the couch a little more cautiously.

She lay on the couch hugging a cotton throw and looking around the candle-lit room. It was so peaceful. The noise had subsided and now all that remained was the wind and the heavy rain. She sipped her wine and closed her eyes, imagining herself in that lovely gown as she walked down the aisle. She smiled, thinking how beautiful everything would be. She could almost smell the flowers blooming all around her as she stood face to face with the man she loved. Then the vision of that old woman's face came back to her and said, "Da man who hold ya heart…he da one that hold da pearl."

A loud knock on the door drew her out of her daydream. Aggravated by the thought that she would have to traipse again across the floor in the dark, she made her way to the door grabbing a candle to help light her way. She opened the door to find Dane standing in front of her. Hannah stared in shock at the sight of him standing there soaking wet. He was leaning on one arm held up against the door frame. He was breathing hard as if he most likely ran from his car in the heavy downpour. She held her candle up to his face and he raised his chin to look at her. She'd never seen him look quite that way before. His eyes were sad and his expression was vacant. Just then the wind blew up around them both and extinguished her candle. It startled her out of the silence, and she took a step back so he could come into the room, but he didn't budge.

The wind shift was blowing rain into her face now and she had to yell over the top of the storm, "Why don't you come inside?"

He took a deep breath and shouted, "I can't! I can't stay. Look, I know you don't want to see me or talk to me, but I just came by to tell you…" he paused. He looked into her eyes. His face was dripping wet. He leaned into the doorway to be closer to her and lowered his voice, "I realized something today. I…I realized that in all this time I forgot…I neglected… to tell you that I love you." He looked into her eyes searching for a response from her. "I know it's the night before your wedding. I know I should have told you months ago. I was so afraid of hurting Paul and his family and—most importantly—you." Hannah continued to stand still and watch him. She decided it was best not to speak. She watched him as he struggled for words to express himself.

"Everything just came together for me today, and I had to get it out tonight. I had to tell you that I fell in love with you the moment I met you at the party. I was instantly jealous that Paul had found you. That's why I was such a jerk to you that night. I didn't think you weren't pretty enough for Paul. I thought you were the most beautiful woman I had ever seen, but I couldn't let Paul know what I was thinking. I certainly couldn't let him think I was jealous! Heck, I've never been jealous of Paul in my life. He's my best friend. I love him and we've always had the utmost respect for each other. And then, there you were, and I didn't know what to think or how to act or what to say.

"It felt like fate stepped in when we were able to grab that time alone together. I felt like I was stealing something that belonged to Paul—something that was never meant for me—but I took it anyway. I had to. I wanted you so badly. I had to know what it was like to hold you and make love to you. But then I was afraid and I felt so guilty. I didn't want to ruin things for you and Paul. I was afraid to tell you that I loved you. I was afraid if I said it, that you wouldn't go back to him. I couldn't take you from him. But then, today an answer just came to me. I realized that I had to tell you that I loved you. That I loved you and that was why I was letting you go. I love you enough to give you the happiness that you deserve with Paul. I want the two of you to be my best friends, just like Paul was before you. The two of you will be one now and I want to be a part of your lives. I want to be your best friend always. I don't want you to avoid me or feel angry or disgusted because of what we did. I want you to release all that and love me, not just as Paul's friend, but as yours. You're going to make a fresh start in your life tomorrow and I wanted to help give that fresh start to you." He stopped and looked at her just staring in silence. The storm had grown quiet. He brushed the raindrops off of his forehead and the tip of his nose. "God, does any of this make sense to you?" He laughed nervously.

Hearing his laugh, Hannah laughed also. Tears fell down her cheeks as she looked at him standing there sopping wet. She wasn't sure why she was crying but the silence between them was unsettling and she knew he was waiting for her to react. She reached up and threw her arms around his neck. She kissed him on the cheek and whispered in his ear, "I love you too, Dane." She intended to pull away quickly, but found it very difficult to let go of him. She'd forgotten how good it felt to be in his arms.

Dane pulled away from her and said, "I have to go, but I want to give you something before I do." He reached into his jacket pocket and pulled out a small box wrapped in white paper and tied with a white ribbon. "I don't know how the saying goes, but I think you have to wear something old and something new on your wedding day. Well, I think this is something really old. Look, Hannah, we had some incredibly intense time together and no one will ever know about it but us. Maybe this is really selfish of me, but I wanted you to have this to remember me...in a good way. Try to remember that something good came out of our meeting. There's something special between us that can't be put into words, but maybe this will be a symbol of it...just between us." She took the box from him and held it in both hands. "Don't open it now," he said. "Open it in the morning, when the sun is out...when the day is new. And we'll start over tomorrow as best friends—you, me, and Paul. If you decide it's wrong to have it then throw it away. I don't want it back. It was never meant for anyone but you."

He took her face in his hands, just as he did that day in the quarter when he brushed her tears away with his thumbs. He caressed her hair as he ran his eyes over every inch of her face as if to commit it to memory. Hannah felt certain he was going to kiss her on her mouth, but perhaps in a moment of strength, he pulled up and kissed her on the forehead. He held his lips there and whispered, "I love you, Hannah. I'll always love you."

"I love you, Dane," she whispered back. She closed her eyes to hold back more tears.

He walked away as the rain continued to fall softly. She watched him with his head down and his hands in the pockets of his jacket walk slowly to his car and drive away. She sluggishly turned to go back inside of the apartment. She couldn't understand why a part of her was hoping that Dane would turn his car around and come running back up to her. She pushed the feeling aside and closed the door.

As she fumbled halfway through the apartment, the lights and the television came back on. She turned everything off and got ready for bed. It was now almost midnight and her beauty sleep plan was fading quickly. She lay in bed in the darkness thinking about her conversation with Dane. She played back every word he had said. He had come there to give her closure and release her from all guilt. Why did she feel so unsettled then? She shifted into a different position in bed trying to calm herself to sleep. She thought again about his words, "I love you enough to let you go." Why did that not make her feel better? Why on the eve of her wedding to the most perfect man, did she still feel some kind of emptiness inside her?

Hannah closed her eyes and tried to fall asleep. Soon her mind was drifting into a series of images. She saw the painting of the woman looking out at the sea. The painting became real and Hannah was there with her on the beach. She watched the young woman quietly sitting there. She saw the man with the pale green eyes sitting in the sand working with his charcoal and sketchpad. Hannah tried to see the woman's face by walking closer to her but all she could ever see was the back of her head. She moved closer again, and then she became the woman sitting on the rock. She turned her head to look back at the artist, but he was gone. Realizing that she was all alone on the beach, she began to cry. Her sobs woke her up. She rolled onto her back and wiped the tears from her eyes.

She thought about the white package Dane had given her that now sat on her vanity. She had promised to wait until morning to open it, but it was making her crazy with curiosity. *It was never meant for anyone but you.* Finally she gave up. There was no way she was going to fall back asleep until she knew what was in it. She pulled the covers back and turned on her bedside lamp. She took the box from her vanity and went back to sit on the edge of the bed. She slowly pulled the ribbon out of its knot, and then gently ripped open the paper. Inside was a soft, red velvet jewelry box. She opened it slowly. She stared down at what was inside with disbelief. The tears began to flow all over again. Hannah knew now what she had to do and it couldn't wait until morning.

Words ran through Hannah's mind as she got into her car and started driving to Paul's house—words that her grandmother had told her years ago and the words of the old woman just a few hours ago. She strained to see through the fog, the rain, and the darkness. She nervously fondled the tiny pendant she wore around her neck as she thought about everything that had happened that night and everything she still needed to do before it was over. "Love is a pearl," the old Creole woman had said. "It lit from within." Four hours ago those words didn't hold any meaning for her. She looked over at the velvet box lying on the seat beside her. She reached over and cracked open the lid to look once again at the gift that Dane had given her. She had tried so hard to deny that her feelings for Dane were real. She was so certain that Paul was her destiny. But now the universe had handed her another sign.

"Da heart know what it want," the old woman had said. "When you see a good thing, you have to grab it while you can. There's no guarantee it will be there later," the artist had told her. After all the night's confusion, things were finally becoming clearer to her, but a mystery still hung over it all. She didn't understand it, and she wasn't sure if she really needed to. What she did know was that she was finally letting her heart guide her. Things were falling together at such a rapid pace, that there was hardly time to think about any of it. It was two o'clock in the morning. and she was out driving in the rain. It was exhilarating! She was so enthralled by the new course of events unfolding before her that she failed to see the light turn red or the truck barreling through the intersection.

6

Julie hung up the phone. Steve's words were still ringing in her ears. She couldn't believe that this was happening. For the last ten months she had been seeing Steve on a regular basis. At first it was every day while he was working on their house addition. Once that was finished, Julie was uncomfortable with him being seen at her house, so they found a hotel downtown. It became "their place" and they had a standing date of Thursday afternoon. Room 208 was the room number their first time there, and so they continued to request that room every time they met. It was kind of a seedy hotel, but she was confident that no one she knew would ever see her there.

She would leave the hotel on Thursday evening after making love to Steve feeling completely fulfilled. On Friday the guilt would begin to creep in as Michael returned from his week on the road. Although there was very little love left in her marriage to Michael, she still knew she was cheating. But after a weekend with him, she would remember why she started seeing Steve in the first place. She felt lonely, old, and desperate. She felt like a captive in her own home—trapped in a mediocre existence with a man who didn't see her as a mate, but as a possession. As soon as Michael was gone on Monday she was fantasizing about Steve and getting wet just thinking about their next meeting. Thursday she would see him. They would make love and everything would be alright again. She realized now she needed him desperately in her life. He was like a drug for her. He made her feel beautiful and alive, desired and sensual, and most of all—free. She hadn't felt that way since she was a teenager. Now—having tasted freedom again—she couldn't imagine living any other way.

Always Thursday and always room 208. Neither the guilt nor the passion seemed to be fading. Thoughts of him ran through her mind all day long. All she could think about was Steve. Julie realized that she was falling deeply in love with him. He was crowding out all other aspects of her life, including her marriage. She wondered how long she could keep up this charade she had with Michael. It was becoming too much for her to carry around every day. At some point, she was going to have to leave her husband. It scared her to think about doing it. She didn't know how she would be able to get away from him if he continued to be so possessive of her. She imagined him hunting her down and strangling her to death. "If I can't have you, no one can!" she could hear him say as he squeezed the last breath out of her body. All she knew now was that she could no longer live in a lie. She wanted to live in the truth and in real love. Steve would be the answer to her problems. He would be the one to rescue her.

She was on the verge of telling him that she was leaving Michael, but she couldn't bring herself to say it. She'd rehearsed it a million times and it always had a happy ending in her mind. She would not suggest that they make any commitment. She would wait to see his reaction. She would give him the opportunity to tell her what she wanted to hear. She thought she knew that his feelings were much like her own, but they had never really discussed it. In fact, they had never said, "I love you." He had told her early on that he was not the type to say things like that. She had accepted it and refused to let herself say it to him. She had to wait until he said it first. Many times while they were making love she put her hand to her mouth to keep from saying it out loud. But nothing could keep her from thinking it. While he was immersed in bringing them both to climax he never knew that she was silently whispering, "I love you. I love you." And it would make her come. She lost her nerve to tell him that afternoon, so it would have to wait another week.

When he didn't show up the following Thursday, she worried about what might have happened to him. She tried to call him, but the office said he was out. A few days went by and her worry turned into fear. She called his office again and asked for him, but they said he was out in the field and asked her to leave a message. She left message after message, day after day, asking him to call her, but with no results. Her fear turned to depression as days turned into weeks. She was an emotional wreck. She had no friends in which to confide. She couldn't talk to her husband. Darkness was taking over. Her mind was filled with possible reasons why he would disappear with no word. Surely he had the guts to at least tell her it was over. Why would he just ignore her? Maybe he was afraid. Maybe he had realized that he was falling in love also, and the feeling had scared him into backing away. That was what she most wanted to believe.

Then the day came when he finally picked up the phone after she called from a phone booth downtown. He told her he didn't think it was a good idea to see each other anymore. He'd had a lot of fun, but it had run its course and they should both move on. She couldn't believe what she was hearing. In a moment of sheer terror that she might never see him again, she let out the words she had promised herself she would never say first. "But I love you, Steve!" she said. "I can't just move on. I love you."

"Julie," he said firmly. "This is not love! It never was and it never will be. Don't delude yourself." He paused, thought and then went on, "I never promised you anything. I never told you I loved you. That's not what I wanted. Look, you're a beautiful, sexy woman. We had fantastic sex, but that's all it was. Now it's over, so don't make it weird."

"If it was so great, why did you stop? Why did you not return my calls?" she asked trembling.

"I don't know. I guess I just got bored," he said. He stayed quiet, and when she gave no reply after a moment, he said, "I gotta go. Take care of yourself." The sound of the line going dead on the other end delivered one last punch to her already broken heart.

A strange hollow feeling came over Julie like a dark fog. She couldn't see or hear anything. She felt cold and small and completely cut off. *I guess I just got bored.* Julie laughed through her tears as she remembered what she was like when she was younger—easily amused with what was right in front of her and just as quickly bored with it. She had never been a lover to him. She'd been a distraction—a disposable distraction. And when she thought about it, she had to admit that's all he had been for her as well. He'd been an escape from her reality. Steve was right. It had never been love.

She stepped out of the phone booth and started walking down the sidewalk. As she passed by the shops, she glanced at her reflection in the windows. She was dressed in a white sleeveless blouse, a denim miniskirt, and wedge sandals. Her long blonde hair lay across her shoulders in curly waves. *I'm still pretty*, she thought to herself. *There must be somebody that still wants me.*

She walked into one of the nicer downtown hotels and sat down at the bar in their lounge. She ordered a glass of white wine and sipped on it until the pain began to subside. Julie thought about all the other men she'd known. She'd given herself to dozens of teenage boys...none that could ever give back what she truly needed. Danny might have loved her, but he had too many commitments back home that were more important. Even her father—the one man whose job it was to love her more than anyone else in this world—never showed it. Michael claimed to love her, but his idea of love had only driven her into another downward spiral. Now she was at the bottom of that drop, and she had no idea how to raise herself out of it.

She sat there brooding over the loss of Steve. He had given her the only hope she had to get away from Michael. What was she to do now? Just then a very tall man in a cowboy hat sat down next to her. He ordered a beer and took a gulp of it before saying in a very deep voice, "You waitin' for anybody?"

Julie stared down at her glass of wine. "No," she said.

He said, "I know this is going to sound like a line, but I gotta say, you are so damn beautiful. What are you doing here alone?"

She looked over at the fingers on his huge hands peeling the label from his bottle while he spoke. She moved her glance to his face and smiled. "Just passing through," she said politely.

"You stayin' here?" he asked.

"No," she said. Julie looked directly into his eyes. "Are you?"

"Yes I am," he said as he polished off the last of his beer. "Would you like to see my room?"

Instantly that familiar warmth ran through her. Julie gulped down the rest of her wine. "Yes," she said. She stepped down off the barstool and followed him to the lobby elevators and up to his room.

As soon as the door closed he wrapped his arms around her and started kissing her. His kisses were rough, very wet, and smelled like beer and cigarettes, but she didn't care. She just wanted to feel wanted. He unbuttoned her blouse and unhooked her bra so he could get his hands on her breasts. He sucked on her nipples so hard that she thought she would cry. She pulled his head away from them and up to her face so he could kiss her some more. They had backed up into the room while they were kissing and now she could feel the bed against the back of her knees. He grabbed the hem of her skirt and pulled it up to expose her panties. He flipped her around and bent her over the bed, pulled her panties down and pushed himself inside of her. She lay there with her face buried in the bedspread and her hips in the air while he slid a rather inadequate penis in and out of her until he came.

When he was finished, he zipped up his fly and sat down on the other bed. He laid his head against the headboard and lit up a cigarette. Julie pulled up her panties and walked to the bathroom. With a washcloth soaked in the hottest water she could stand, she washed off the semen that was running down her legs and into her sandals. She washed her hands, wiped off the mascara that had smeared under her eyes, straightened her clothes, and walked back out of the bathroom.

As she reached for the door into the hallway, he said, "I'll be in town again next week."

Julie opened the door and looked back at him. She said. "I won't." She turned back around and headed for the elevator and home.

7

Hannah slammed on her brakes in time to miss the truck. Her heart was pounding and her mind was reeling from the thought of the disaster she had just avoided. The jolt made her stop and realize that she had been moving too quickly without considering all that was at stake. She sat there for a moment or two just reflecting on what she was doing. As much as she wanted to follow her heart, she was now reminded that there was more in play here than just her feelings. She thought back to what Dane had told her earlier that night. He had been so unselfish by stepping out of the way to let her be with Paul. He loved both of them too much to ever hurt either of them. Now she realized that her plan of action tonight would just be undoing Dane's kindness. She couldn't ruin the beauty of the friendship between Paul and Dane. They had known each other since they were children. They had a bond so great that it was meant to last forever. In this case— where two lives are deeply intertwined—to hurt one man was to hurt them both. To love one man was to love them both. Because hurting them was not an option, she had to find a way to love them.

Hannah pulled her car over on the side of the street just a few blocks down from Paul's house. She dug around in the glove box until she found a pen and something to write on. She scratched out a note on the backside of an envelope. She didn't even have to think of what to say. The words poured out of her as if they had been written years ago and she was just now remembering them. The rain continued to fall as she opened her car door. She quickly scrambled up the steps of Paul's house and placed the note inside the storm door. She ran back to her car and drove away. When she arrived back at the apartment, she packed her things, and then checked into a hotel room for the night. She thought about going back to Mississippi, but she wasn't ready to give up her job that easily. She decided to stay in town for a little while until her heart told her what her next move would be.

She lay there under the covers of a king-size bed on the eighth floor of a downtown hotel. For once tonight she was truly happy and at peace. She was content with the decision she had made and the actions she had taken. It was nearly four o'clock. She thought about Paul's family waking up soon to get ready for a wedding only to discover her note. She pictured Paul's disappointed face reading it over and over, trying to understand why she would do this to him at the last minute. Then she said a prayer that he would eventually forgive her. Maybe someday he would realize that this was the best thing that she could have done for them all.

Paul,
I love you so dearly, and it hurts me so much to do this to you. I'm afraid I can't marry you. You have been the greatest friend to me. Your family has welcomed me as if I am one of their own. I have no good reason to call this off, except that I realized tonight that I haven't given you my whole heart. I cannot let you enter into a commitment like marriage to someone who cannot fully commit herself to you in return. Please forgive me, darling, for the embarrassment I am causing you and your family! Please don't hate me! I hope someday you will understand that I loved you enough to let you go.
Hannah

8

All my life, my heart has yearned for a thing I cannot name.

–Andre Breton

Julie lay on a raft in her new pool that was now enclosed inside her beautiful screened-in pool room. The sun felt good as it streamed in through the skylight above her. She closed her eyes and concentrated on the warmth. It was comforting. She raised her head to take another sip of her white wine and then laid her head back down. Floating there in a circle in her yellow bikini and feeling the heat on her belly, she thought back to the night when her baby was born. She held that beautiful little girl in her arms for the first time, marveling at her perfection. She could still see those delicate little fingers and toes, her perfect mouth, and her green eyes…Danny's eyes. As she lay on the kitchen floor of her apartment cradling her newborn, she thanked God that the abortion had not been successful. She cried while her heart overflowed with joy that this baby girl had not given up on her. *Oh Danny*, she thought. *If you could only have seen what a wonderful thing our love made.*

She took the last sip of her wine and laid it on the side of the pool. She pushed herself away from the edge so she was floating in the middle. The room was warm, and the smell of chlorine filled the air. Her head was getting lighter. She smiled as she settled into this relaxed state. The pills she took earlier were finally starting to work. *How many had she taken?* She tried to count them in her mind. *Two...four...six...was it six? No...eight...maybe ten...* She glanced up at the clock. Michael would be home in a couple of hours.

Julie closed her eyes. She felt really good now, like she was floating on air. Thoughts of her mother entered her mind just then. She pictured her mother in the kitchen, standing over the sink, staring out the window with a look of sadness and desperation in her eyes. Julie thought now she finally understood her mother's mind. She realized the depth of darkness that comes with the absence of love. And in that moment of clarity, she stopped hating her mother. Instead she took pity on her unhappiness. How strong her mother had been to have kept going all those years, living with unfathomable grief and a man she didn't love—always pushing forward just to make sure her daughter had some kind of life.

Julie cried for her mother's sorrow but even more in shame of her own weakness. She had been given many chances, but had never taken the path of strength. All Julie had ever wanted was to be loved—truly loved. She'd spent her whole life searching for it, but managed to walk down too many wrong roads to get it. She couldn't blame anyone but herself for her sadness. She thought she'd found the fairy tale with Michael and all she'd really found was a castle in which to lock herself up for eternity. Her need for security, admiration and acceptance had created the walls that were her fortress. But now those things meant nothing to her.

She wondered how he would find her. *Would she be lying peacefully on the raft like she was now with her hands folded gracefully at her waist? Would she slip off when she lost consciousness and Michael would find her floating face down in the water, like in that old movie? What was the name of that movie?* She couldn't think anymore. Her mind was dizzy. It didn't really matter anyway. There was no turning back now.

The sun was no longer overhead and the room was beginning to cool down. The warmth and peacefulness she felt earlier was gone. She tried to open her eyes, but she couldn't. Everything was dark. The cold and the blackness began to frighten her, and she tried to cry out, "I'm scared! Someone help me!" But just as in her worst nightmares, her mouth could not make the words. *Don't cry*, she thought to herself. *Soon it will be over.* She would have escaped the only way she knew how. *Ha!* She thought how ironic it was that the last gift Michael gave her would be her doorway out of his life for good. She was finally leaving…she would soon be free!

Her thoughts drifted back in time, and she saw herself on that warm day in June when she walked up the steps of a front porch and placed the basket with her sleeping little girl at the door. She peeked inside the blanket to get one last look at the tiny person lying there. She wanted to see her pale green eyes just once more—to see Danny's life in her, but she couldn't take a chance on waking her. One last kiss goodbye and then she walked away as quickly as possible. She felt the tears come to her eyes, and her heart ached painfully as she made her way to the bus stop and the ride back to Florida.

Julie smiled as she remembered, and tears streamed down her cheeks as she drifted off into sleep. *I did the right thing. There was nothing more I could give you, Baby Girl. I had to let you go. Don't cry. Don't look back and don't cry.*

9

After David's death, Helen became severely withdrawn. She could not attend school. She would barely eat. Her parents sent her to a mental hospital in Topeka in the hope that she would recover and come back to them as she used to be. Although the doctors said that she was ready to come back, upon her return home she experienced horrible night terrors. Frightened that she might relapse and never recover, her parents sent her to a private girls' school in Memphis to let her finish high school.

After she graduated, she and a girlfriend from school shared an apartment not far from a women's clothing boutique where Helen found a job. Although Helen had never been one for fashion, she had an attractive, tall, thin figure and clothes hung well on her. The store's owner took advantage of Helen's looks and used her often to model their newest arrivals, which boosted sales and earned Helen an extra commission. Being in sales forced Helen to open up more, and she learned to converse with the general public. She became very skilled at what she did. She was bright, friendly, and very persuasive. The regular customers adored her. The new customers flocked to her for advice. No one would ever know that behind her lovely, charming smile was a sad, empty little girl on an island far away who sat waiting for the love of her life to come back to her. She didn't want anyone to know about it. She'd spent years learning to hide it. But at night when she was alone in her bed, she still longed for him.

Two doors down from her shop was a flooring store. The owner's name was Frank Mills. He was fifteen years older than she was. He'd been married before, but his wife had died in a car accident a few years earlier. She met him at the lunch counter in the drugstore downtown. He was eating a sandwich and watching the television behind the counter. She was having lunch with her girlfriend a few seats down from him. Her friend pointed out to Helen that this man kept looking over at her. Helen had no interest in meeting any man and quickly dismissed it. Her friend, however, escalated the situation by introducing herself and Helen to him. Frank admitted that he'd seen her pass by his shop every morning on her way to work and that was why he kept glancing over at her. At the coaxing of her friend, they continued to carry on a conversation. After that day, he would always say hello to her as she passed by in the mornings. And she would say hello back. This went on for several weeks. One day Frank worked up the nerve to ask her to have dinner with him and she accepted.

As much as Helen hated the thought of ever being with someone other than David, she had to admit that Frank was attractive. He had dark brown eyes, olive skin, and coal black hair that he wore slicked back neatly. She enjoyed going out with him, because he was quiet— a little sad— and always a gentleman. He made her feel safe, so when he asked her to marry him, she accepted. It was not a marriage for love, but more for convenience. He was looking for someone to make a home for him. She needed a reason to not return home. She could never really love him—not the way she loved David. Frank knew that and accepted it. He had no interest in a romance. He simply needed a wife. In exchange for that he promised to take care of her so that she would never have to go back to her family.

Helen became pregnant a year after they were married. It was mostly unexpected since she had only been with Frank once. He had come home intoxicated one night as she was getting ready for bed. In his drunken state he decided to approach her as she stood there in her slip. He awkwardly put his hand up to caress her shoulder and then put his lips on her mouth. Not knowing how she should behave, she allowed him to kiss her. His kisses were soft and gentle, and he looked so sad and lonely. She knew it was her responsibility as his wife to give him the comfort that he needed and so she let him make love to her that night. Although he had been very patient and tender, it had been a complete disappointment for her. When it was over, Helen told him she could never do it again.

She had always wanted children, but the birth of her daughter triggered painful emotions that had been lying dormant within her. Seeing her little girl as she went from a toddler to a young woman brought back memories of her own childhood and the horror that ended it. Through the years she became more and more withdrawn. Her resentment of her husband grew as her feelings of grief resurfaced. He offered no assistance or emotional support to Helen, which only pushed them further apart. There was no laughter, no love, and no joy. Every dream that Helen had of how her family would someday be was crushed by reality.

Frank turned to drinking as life at home became more stressful. Eventually he didn't even come home. He spent his evenings at the corner bar and slept at the shop. Most every night Helen cried herself to sleep after she'd put her daughter to bed. She felt so lost and confused. She was trying to make a life for herself but this was no life at all. Now she had a child to think about. She couldn't just walk away. She would lie in her bed and wonder if David would do as he had promised and come for her—to take her out of this darkness she was living in.

As the years passed by, Helen became angry and bitter. She was mad at David for leaving her in a world that was so empty. She did what she could to provide a home for her daughter with an absent husband and father. It was a miserable existence for them all, but she could not see a way out of it. They went through the motions of being a family without ever connecting with each other.

When Frank fell ill with cancer, she did her best to take care of him until he died. It was hard to see him suffer through his disease. Despite the lack of love, Helen still cared for him and hated to see him in such pain. He had never been mean or abusive. His greatest harm had been his absence in their lives. Once he was gone, it didn't really make a noticeable difference in their household. She'd long grown used to the quiet emptiness of their life.

What hurt the most was when her daughter left home at the age of eighteen. Helen could hardly blame her for wanting to find something better, but she worried about her wandering around in such a cold world alone. Julie had been a beautiful little girl and an exceptionally attractive teenager, but she was troubled. She had taken after her father when it came to keeping her emotional distance. Just as it had been with Frank, Helen felt as if she could never break through the barrier. She wished she could have been a better mother to her. She wondered if she and Frank had given her the guidance she needed to make a life for herself. Now it was too late.

10

There is no disguise which can hide love for long where it exists, or simulate it where it does not.

— *François de La Rochefoucauld*

Hannah had already taken a week's vacation from her job for the wedding, so it gave her some time to put her life in order. Before she did anything, though, she went to see Nana. She had to explain what had transpired the night before the wedding and why she felt compelled to cancel. There were also things that Hannah needed to understand. No one else knew the answers but her grandmother. They went back to Jackson, and Hannah returned a few days later to shop for a place to live. It didn't take long to find a house to rent in Metairie. She thought it might be best to get out of the city—less chances to run into Paul or Dane. She loved New Orleans and she just wasn't ready to move away. Something told her that she belonged here, so she stayed.

The day she started back to work, Hannah found Paul sitting on the steps of her building. She approached him cautiously as he stood up. He asked if they could have a cup of coffee together and she agreed. She figured she owed him at least that much after leaving him hanging on the day of their wedding.

It was a warm day for November, so they took advantage of the sunshine and found a table outside at a nearby café. Hannah was nervous. She couldn't read Paul's face to tell if he was angry or not. She took a deep breath, blew on her hot coffee and took a sip, waiting for Paul to begin the conversation.

"Are you going home for the holidays?" Paul asked.

It wasn't exactly the question she was anticipating from him. She had to stop and think about the answer. "Actually yes, I really need to spend some time with Nana," Hannah said. She kept looking off into the distance. She was starting to wish she hadn't gone with him. She'd been quite prepared mentally for this conversation—or so she thought. Now that she was facing him she was losing her nerve. She took another sip of her coffee and tried to focus on the taste of the vanilla and cinnamon in it to calm her anxiety. She wrapped her trembling hands around the cup in the hope that the heat of the coffee would stop them from shaking. She knew eventually he would broach the subject and she hoped she would find the right words.

"Wait till you see it here at Christmas," said Paul. "The decorations everywhere are so cool. And New Year's...New Year's Eve is just the best." He smiled awkwardly at her. He could see he was getting nowhere with small talk, so he jumped right in. "Hannah," he said as he leaned across the table to be closer to her. "I've read your note a hundred times. I've gone over everything in my head. I don't know for sure why you called off our wedding, but I just want to say that if it's something I did, I'm really sorry. I know when we came down here we both were so caught up in starting our careers...me especially. I don't feel like I paid enough attention to you. I should have. It was a time when we both should have been so...so into each other. It should have been one of the most romantic times of our relationship, but it wasn't."

"That should tell you something right there, Paul." Hannah looked into his eyes. "It should have been the *best* time of our lives, but it wasn't." She held his stare for a few seconds and then continued. "I'm not complaining and I'm not blaming you. I'm just saying that with everything we had going for us, something was missing."

"Yeah, I guess you're right," he said. "That should have been a magical time for us, and if we didn't have it going into the marriage, how would we ever find it later, huh?"

"Yes," Hannah said sadly. "But, Paul, you're not the cause for what was missing. I don't want you to get the wrong impression. I don't hold anything against you. I still love you and I want to be friends if we can. You are a great person and I would hate for you to disappear altogether from my life."

"Thank you," he said. Paul took a deep breath, almost as if he were cleansing himself of all the discomfort he'd been feeling for the last few weeks. He paused for a moment to think before he asked, "Have you seen Dane?"

Hannah blushed. "No. Why?"

"No reason. I just wondered if he tried to get in touch with you. He knew how hard this was for me. He tried not to show it but I think he was just as upset as I was. That's the thing about Dane and me. We've been like brothers to each other. We've been through everything together. Sometimes it's hard to tell where he ends and I begin. We've always shared everything." He looked up at Hannah. She tried hard to keep her feelings out of her face, but she could feel the blood in her cheeks. She hoped Paul wouldn't notice.

"Well," said Paul. "I guess we better get going if we want to keep our jobs!" He laughed.

They both stood up and started walking back to her building. When they reached it, Paul turned and put his arms around Hannah and kissed her lightly on the cheek. "Thanks for meeting with me. I don't want any animosity between us. I hope we can always be friends. I'll always love you, Hannah."

"Thank you, Paul. I have a feeling we always will be friends." Hannah hugged him one more time and the two parted. It was such a relief to have it behind her. She walked into work ready to take on the day and the rest of her life.

Hannah didn't see or hear from Paul again for a while. She went home to see Nana for Thanksgiving. She was glad to be reconnecting with her. She felt like she had neglected her grandmother over the last year, spending so much time with Paul and trying to establish a new home. It was like old times with just the two of them again.

A few days before Christmas, Paul called her. He said he hoped she meant what she said about them remaining friends and he wondered what she was doing for New Year's Eve. It was the greatest time to be in New Orleans and he wanted so much to celebrate the new millennium with her and about eighty-thousand other people downtown. Hannah laughed at his humorous approach, and accepted his invitation.

When the last day of December actually came, she started having hesitations about her plans. She stood at the window of her apartment looking out at the cold, misty, gray day. She was holding a hot cup of tea to take off the chill. All she really wanted to do that night was curl up on the couch in a warm blanket and watch the ball drop in Times Square. But New Year's Eve can be a rough night to spend alone. It would be good for her to get out. Other than a happy hour with friends at work, she hadn't been anywhere socially in a very long time. At least she was going to be there with a friend and no romantic expectations or awkward moments to anticipate.

She had been thinking about Dane too. She missed him terribly. The holidays had made her long to be with the man she loved. She knew now that Dane was that man, but she didn't see how they could ever be together. While she was at home, she had told her grandmother the whole story about meeting Dane and how she had been unsure about everything until the night he showed up in the rain. She told her about the wedding gift he had given her. That's when her grandmother smiled and said, "Hannah, you know what your heart wants. Follow your heart or you'll never be happy." But Hannah was still too afraid of how her actions might hurt others. She just wasn't ready to make a move. Even if Paul was content with their newly formed friendship, she was sure it would kill him to see his best friend in a relationship with her. If it was meant to be then something would open the door for them, she was certain.

She slipped on a pink turtleneck sweater and jeans. She brushed her hair and touched up her makeup. Standing in front of her mirror putting on her lipstick, she couldn't help but feel a little déjà vu happening. She thought about the many times she had stood in front of her mirror getting ready for a date with Paul. Hopefully this wasn't a mistake. The doorbell rang. Too late to wonder! It was then that she realized she was just a little bit nervous. Hannah took a deep breath and went to the door.

Paul was standing at her doorstep looking very happy. She couldn't remember the last time she'd seen him look that way. He told her she looked beautiful, and she thanked him as he helped her put on her coat. They decided to grab some dinner before heading downtown. Paul took her to a nice Italian restaurant, and they arrived in Jackson Square just as the crowds began to thicken.

Hannah looked around at the buildings in the French Quarter. Paul had been right about the decorations. It was so beautiful to see the old shops and houses decked out with greenery and red ribbons, strings of Christmas lights, angels made out of wire and tinsel, ornaments and beads threaded through wrought iron railings. It was indicative of the incredibly unique style that one could only find in New Orleans. The energy was growing with the throngs of people waiting to ring in a new year, a new decade, and a new century all with the tiny movement of a hand on a clock. It was becoming a sea of silly hats, noisemakers, flags, and large containers of alcohol. Hannah was beginning to feel pushed and pulled as their surroundings grew tighter. Paul warned her that the crowd would get so dense by midnight that it would be nearly impossible to take even a few steps. He advised her to hold his hand tightly, so that they would not get separated. She gladly took his hand and he smiled at her. "I'm so glad I could bring you here tonight. I think you're really going to like it," he said. "We should try to get up the hill so we can see the fireworks at midnight." They tried their best to make their way closer to the riverfront. Paul pulled Hannah along through the swarms of highly intoxicated partiers. "C'mon! It's almost time!" Paul yelled to her as he tugged her hand.

"Ten…nine…eight…" The countdown was beginning. Hannah tried to keep up with Paul and still watch all the festivities going on around her. It was magical. "Six…five…four…" the crowd roared. Just then Hannah's hand slipped out of her glove and Paul's grip. She turned quickly to look for him, but she couldn't see him with the darkness and mobs of people in front of her. She pushed and forced her way through them working her way toward the riverfront. It was one second before midnight, and she was lost! She strained to see over the crowd and to find Paul's face. Just then a hand grabbed hers. *Thank God!* She squeezed his hand and allowed him to pull her forward. But when she was finally through, it wasn't Paul's face that she saw. It was Dane's! She looked at him with complete disbelief and bewilderment. Dane put his arms around her and kissed her just as the first fireworks shot above their heads. "Happy New Year!" the multitudes yelled.

Dane's lips on hers felt so good. Hannah didn't want the moment to end. She had missed his warm kisses and his arms around her body. Their lips unlocked and she hugged him tightly against her. "Happy New Year, baby," Dane said.

With her eyes still closed and her face up to his cheek, she said, "Oh, my love, is this really real?" She opened her eyes to see Paul standing behind Dane. He was smiling. Then he turned and disappeared into the crowd as if he'd slipped behind a curtain.

"Paul!" Hannah yelled. But he didn't come back.

Dane let go of her a little so he could see her face. "It's okay," he said reassuringly. "He knows everything. He figured it out actually." He held her close to him again and said, "God, I've missed you! There's so much I need to tell you." Dane looked around at all the people. It was so loud, hardly a place for a conversation. "Hey, let's get out of here…if we can!" he yelled.

Hannah let him lead her to his car. He barely said a word to her on the drive home. He just held her hand and kept looking over at her as if he couldn't quite believe what he was seeing. Hannah couldn't believe it either. Her mind was racing with a million different questions. She felt confused and anxious, but most of all she felt joy—like she'd never known in her life.

As they sat on his living room sofa, Dane explained that Paul and he had gotten together over Christmas. Paul mentioned that he'd had coffee with Hannah. When he saw the look on Dane's face at the mention of her name—the same look he'd seen on Hannah's face when he'd mentioned Dane—he knew there was something between them. He questioned Dane until he finally confessed his feelings for Hannah. He'd been a little angry at first, but then he realized that being mad at them would not accomplish anything. Dane told Paul that he was just as shocked as he was when Hannah called off the wedding. Being the friend and brother that he had always been to Dane, Paul lovingly suggested that they find a way to get him back with Hannah. "Just like you, Dane, I can't be happy at the expense of the two people I love most," Paul had said to him.

"And that's when we decided to cook up this New Year's Eve thing," said Dane. "I tell you, Hannah, I've never felt so much relief as that day. Being able to come clean with Paul and admit my feelings for you…it was such a relief." Dane looked down at the necklace Hannah was wearing and said, "I see you kept the necklace. It's nice to see you wearing it. I hoped you hadn't thrown it away."

Hannah reached down and took the silver heart pendant and held it between two fingers. She said, "Dane, you didn't give me this necklace." She laughed.

"What?" Dane asked. "Yes I did! I gave you that necklace the night before your wedding."

Hannah laughed again at his confusion. "Yes, you did give me a necklace that looked just like this one the night before my wedding. However, my grandmother gave me *this* necklace when I left for college. The necklace you gave me is still in the box at home. I never took it out. When I opened your present that night and saw that you had given me the necklace that was identical to the one she gave me, I knew the universe was trying to tell me something. Dane, this necklace was very important to my grandmother, and so was its twin. She always felt like they had some kind of magic in them."

Dane looked at her with a stunned expression. "I think your grandmother is right," he said slowly. "The day before your wedding Paul and I went out for a boat ride. He was talking nonstop about you and it was making me crazy. I wanted so badly to tell Paul how I felt about you, but I knew I couldn't. He was so happy. It just frustrated the hell out of me. Not to see him happy but to be so torn between his happiness and my own. Then Paul reminded me how we used to go boating all the time when we were kids and how we hadn't been out together like that in years. He pulled a picture out of his wallet. It was badly worn and creased but you could still see it was a picture of us when we were boys. We'd been out on his parents' boat and his mother had snapped the picture of us. She'd made two prints and given one to each of us. Apparently Paul had carried his picture in his wallet all these years. Seeing that picture reminded me again of how much our friendship meant to him. I calmed down and relaxed enough to enjoy the rest of the afternoon.

"When I got home later I went straight up to my room. I knew I had a copy of that photograph somewhere. I opened every drawer of my dressers, night stands, searching for it. The last drawer I opened was a little side drawer of the vanity. Sure enough, among a stack of photographs there was the picture of Paul and me. We were twelve. We were in our swimsuits, holding fishing rods and Paul had his arm around my shoulder. My eyes welled up with tears looking at it, remembering the good times we'd had. I laid the picture down to wipe my eyes and that's when I noticed something shiny inside the drawer catch the light.

"Now, I've had this bedroom set since I bought it at an auction in Jackson last year. I'd been through every drawer, cleaned everything out before I brought it inside the house. All of a sudden, I see this necklace—this silver heart necklace—wedged in the corner of this drawer. I don't know how I could have missed it earlier, but it certainly had to have been in there when I bought the furniture, because I'd never seen it before. So I pull it out of the drawer and I'm staring at it—thinking how beautiful it is—and all I could think about was you. I don't know what or why, but something told me that I needed to give that necklace to you. I saw it as a chance for me to make peace with you before your big day so we could start over right. That's when everything I told you that night just started revealing itself to me. And so I wrapped it up and went to see you. Your grandmother is definitely right, Hannah. There is something magical about those necklaces."

Hannah had been quiet the entire time he told his tale. Now she knew whose furniture was sitting upstairs in Dane's bedroom. She shivered to think of how everything had come together in this way. "I don't know if the magic is in the necklaces, Dane. I think it's in us."

"But why didn't you come back and tell me that night after you first opened it?" Dane asked.

"I had every intention of telling you that night before the wedding. I was on my way to your house as soon as I broke up with Paul, but then I realized that it wasn't the right way to handle the situation. It wasn't the right time. I had to wait," Hannah said. "That's the thing about love. My Nana used to tell me that sometimes you just have to be patient and still. You have to wait and trust your heart that it will come. And it did…and you did…and here we are."

Dane leaned toward Hannah, took her by the shoulders and gently laid her down on the couch below them. His hands brushed the hair from her face as he lay on top of her. "I guess you were right to wait, but now that you're here, I don't want to wait anymore," he whispered. Then he pressed his lips to hers in a lingering kiss. "How about I show you my bedroom?" he said smiling.

11

Just a year after Julie left home, Helen went to her front door to answer the bell and found a bundle in a basket on the porch with a note on top. The note said:

I can't take care of this. Try to do a better job with it than you did with me.

Helen pulled the blanket apart to reveal a tiny baby girl. The note was from Julie, which meant this child was her granddaughter. Of course, Helen would never know the mystery of how that life entered the world. It was the last she would ever hear from Julie.

Something about that little baby's face looking up at Helen—helpless and longing for love—struck a chord in her heart. A tiny light came into Helen's world that day—small but so bright—it pierced through her darkness. Helen saw she was being given a second chance at parenting. She could become a better grandmother than she had been a mother. She picked that baby up and cradled her in her arms. She would love this child and give her the life that Julie never had. She named the baby Hannah.

When her mother died, Helen inherited the house back in Jackson. Ready for a fresh start, she decided to move Hannah back to Mississippi to live in her childhood home. Before they left Tennessee, Helen tried to find Julie one more time. She wanted her to know where she could find Hannah in case she ever had the desire. But there was no trail anywhere to find her. She tried hospital records in the area hoping to find out where Hannah had been born, but there was nothing to be found.

It was hard for Helen at first to face the memories of her last days in that house, but she also knew it was time to move forward if she was going to make a good life for Hannah. To help her start over, she renovated the entire house. By the time she was finished it was a beautiful, bright home with all modern conveniences. It was the happy home that Helen had always wanted but didn't think was possible. After years of hiding in the shadows, she now saw that chasing away old demons was just like sweeping away the dust. You just had to know how to confront them. She still thought about David every day, but not with sadness. Now that she was home again, she felt him closer to her. Hope returned that he might one day come back just as he said he would. She would lie awake in her bed at night and talk to him, like she did when she was younger. She would tell him all about Hannah and how much she wanted him to know her. "Please come back to me David. I'll be here waiting," she would say to him before falling asleep.

Hannah was growing into a young girl quickly. Although she was almost as pretty, Hannah was very different from Julie. She was a kind-hearted and sweet little girl. Helen found it easy to raise her. She kept her entertained with stories of when she was a little girl. She told Hannah all about the adventures she and David had on "David's Island" and the king that saved her from the dragons. Hannah's big green eyes would look up at her grandmother and she would ask, "Nana, can we go? I want to see David's Island!" Helen would laugh and tell her, "Close your eyes, Hannah Girl, and sail away in your boat to David's Island. That's the only way to get there." Hannah obediently followed instruction and sailed off quickly to sleep.

The years rushed by for them. Hannah passed from childhood to her awkward teenage years and then into a beautiful young woman. Just before she left for her first semester of college, Helen gave her a little velvet box wrapped in pink and yellow paper. As Hannah was unwrapping her gift, Helen told her the story of two women—both expecting their first child—who met in a coffee shop when each noticed the other wearing identical necklaces. Inside the box was a silver filigree heart with a tiny pearl in the center on a delicate silver chain. She told her about a friendship and ultimately a love that grew between a boy and a girl—a love so strong that nothing could ever destroy it—not even death.

Hannah cried as her grandmother related this tragic story to her, but Helen had told her that she shouldn't cry. She told her that she was giving her the necklace to remind her that she should never give up hope or settle for anyone less than the love of her life. "When you find him, you will know. And this necklace will remind you of that until then," she said.

"But it's still so sad for you, Nana! I didn't realize that all this time…all those years…you've been missing him," Hannah said. "How hard it must have been for you to come back to this house and face all those terrible memories! And here I am getting ready to go off to college to leave you here alone again. Maybe I shouldn't go just yet."

Helen looked lovingly at her sweet unselfish granddaughter. "Hannah, it's time for you to go. I will be fine. There was a time—for a long time—I had given up. I lived in darkness, and I let it take over my life. Then you came along. You brought me back to life and now I realize that there's still hope. My life isn't over yet, Hannah. There's still a chance that he will find me." Helen smiled at her and then held Hannah tightly in her arms and said, "Just promise me that you'll hold onto the hope. Don't let yourself get lost in the dark like I did. It's so hard to find your way back, my darling."

Hannah left for college the following week. Now Helen was faced with the challenge of being strong all by herself again. She had to back up all her promises to Hannah with real action. It was a little scary at first—being on her own after all those years. But when she looked back over her life, she realized that she'd never really had anyone else but herself to rely on all along. She'd run a household, raised a daughter and a granddaughter basically by herself. It gave her a whole new perspective and the courage she needed to keep going. She kept herself busy by volunteering with a local crisis center. She liked to think she could make a difference in some poor frightened child's life. Every little boy she saw reminded her of David. *If only there had been someone to help him and his mother…if only*, she thought.

On her own, Helen began to sift through the memories of when it had been just David and her in their own little world. She took long walks and retraced their childhood footsteps to the river. She sat alone in the grass and felt the warm sun on her face, remembering the days when they were the only two people in the world. She felt younger than she had in years, and she sensed that it was because David was more near to her. She could feel him around her in everything she did. Every night she still lay in bed thinking about him. "I'm still here, David," she would say quietly as she drifted off to sleep. "I'm waiting for you. Please find me."

All the time that Helen was becoming more childlike and learning to trust in the way her life was unfolding, Hannah was becoming a woman. She was delighted when Hannah announced her engagement to Paul and shocked when she called off the wedding. She'd never known her granddaughter to be so indecisive. But when Hannah came to her that next day to show her the necklace that Dane had given her, it all made perfect sense. It was more than coincidence that Dane would give Hannah a necklace identical to the one she had—the one that once belonged to David's mother. Seeing both pendants together also gave Helen hope that everything was falling together just as it should. Not just for Hannah, but for David and her as well. The magic of the necklaces was a mystery that might never be solved, but Helen told Hannah that she had done the right thing. She could also see that Hannah was without a doubt deeply in love with Dane. It was hard to watch her struggle with her feelings and the complications that came with her involvement with these two men, but she also knew that time and patience would allow love to find its way.

Six months later on a sunny summer day Helen escorted Hannah down the length of the dock that stretched out over the Mississippi River at Dane's boat house. Hannah was dressed in a white satin gown beautifully embroidered and studded with tiny pearls. Around her neck she wore two identical silver filigree hearts on a silver chain. She was looking straight ahead to the end of the dock where the love of her life stood, waiting to start their life together. Helen stood by and listened to Hannah and Dane exchanging vows. She felt a lump rise up in her throat and tears of happiness come to her eyes. She wished Julie could be with them to see how amazing her daughter had turned out. As happy as she was to have been given the opportunity to raise Hannah, she still felt such deep regret at all her daughter had missed. Hannah looked radiant as she looked into Dane's eyes and they kissed for the first time as husband and wife. *Our hearts found a home in these two, David*, she thought quietly to herself.

12

True love is like ghosts, which everyone talks about and few have seen. — François de La Rochefoucauld

Another Halloween was upon her, and Helen stepped out of the movie theater. It was an exceptionally warm night. She had no trick-or-treaters in her house anymore and had little interest in staying at home to hand out candy. She decided to stay cool and treat herself to the newest picture that had just been released. It was a romantic drama that had a happy ending but did not really leave her feeling happy. She felt uneasy that night. She couldn't put her finger on it, but something was happening. Maybe it was just the seasons about to change. There was definitely energy in the air.

As she took her first step out of the theater that night, she heard the rumble of thunder. The wind was beginning to gust as well. She watched as women held on to their skirt hems with one hand and onto their dates with the other as they pushed on through it. Trash skidded past her as she paused for a moment to remember where she had parked her car. Helen was now sixty-seven. She still looked like she was fifty, but she felt like a fumbling old woman tonight struggling to remember which direction to walk. *Right...no left...I parked on the corner of Elm and Fifth...not Madison.* Helen turned to her left and as she began down the sidewalk, she felt the first raindrops hit her face. Now she was angry with herself for not bringing an umbrella.

A brilliant bolt of lightning flashed and then the terrible clap of thunder followed. *There was a time*, she thought with a smile, *when I wouldn't be caught dead in weather like this.* She remembered her tremendous fear of storms when she was young. After David died they didn't seem to bother her anymore. Nothing at all had ever felt as overwhelming or frightening to Helen after he was gone. Tonight's weather was no different. In fact she almost enjoyed the anticipation of the storm. There was electricity in the air and that meant a possibility for change. Anything could happen.

The rain was now picking up, and she was getting drenched. She was looking down at her dress that was soaked when a hand reached out in the darkness grabbing her arm and pulling her under an awning. Although she was startled she was grateful to have some shelter. She looked up, smiled and said, "Thank you," to the stranger she couldn't see. She thought it odd that he didn't respond to her, but what she found the most puzzling was that he was holding her hand. She looked down at the gentleman's warm hand holding hers. She wasn't quite sure how to ask for her hand back. She tried to just let go, but he held firm. Looking up again, she struggled to see his face, but it was too dark. Just then a lightning bolt came down so close and with such intensity that it lit up the street brighter than the sun could on any given summer day. It was more than Helen could take. She scrunched her eyes tightly together. Not only did she squeeze this stranger's hand tightly, but took her other hand and grabbed the sleeve of his coat, while burying her face in the fabric. She couldn't believe how childish she was behaving, but for the first time in a long time she was really afraid.

"It's okay, Helen. I'll protect you," said the stranger.

Upon hearing those words, Helen's eyes opened wide. Her heart stopped for a second, then began to pound loudly in her chest. She knew those words. Although she hadn't heard them in many years, they came back to her in an instant. Helen pulled her face from his coat and looked back up at him. She ran her right hand over the soft fabric of his overcoat up to his cheek. She looked up into the darkness and in a leap of faith, she said softly, "David."

The stranger turned slightly and bent down towards Helen until the light from the sign next door revealed his face. He smiled at her gently and said, "The name is Jack Dunham. I'm sorry that I'm not who you thought I was. I just saw you walking by in the midst of the storm, and I felt like I had to pull you into safety. I hope I didn't frighten you." He continued to look directly into Helen's eyes. She could not stop searching his face. Her eyes traced every feature, seeking the familiarity that she had found in his words, but there wasn't any. She felt foolish for her strange behavior, but at the same time she felt compelled to press for resolution.

"Then why did you call me Helen? Why did you say 'It's okay *Helen*?' " she asked seriously as she stared back at him desperately seeking an explanation.

"Did I? But how could I?" the stranger said. He continued to smile at her. Helen felt as though he understood what she was thinking and feeling. The stranger's eyes looked up for a moment to see the light of the sign next door and then back to Helen's face. He said, "I know we've just met, but I'm new in town and you're the first person I've held in my arms since I arrived. I figure that makes you my best friend." He smiled a little bigger and paused to see how Helen would react. Helen's eyes popped at his words. She hadn't realized that all this time he had been holding her in his arms. Tears began to overflow her eyes, and he took out a handkerchief to carefully dab them off her cheeks. "Please don't cry. I didn't mean to frighten you... I'm sorry...Helen. That is your name, right? Helen?"

Helen swallowed so she could move her mouth again. It had gone dry after having left it hanging open so long. "Yes, my name is Helen," she said very delicately. She couldn't stop her tears. They were not tears out of fear or happiness, but confusion. She wanted so badly to understand what was happening to her. Her heart was telling her something that her mind would not accept.

When he realized that he was staring at her for far too long in silence, he quickly moved his eyes again above Helen's head to the sign on the café next door. "Well, Helen, I see Mary's Café is still open. Would you be interested in having a cup of coffee with me?" He stopped for a moment and thought. "You know what sounds even better?" He chuckled to himself and shook his head. "Gosh, I haven't had one in such a long time, but a chocolate milkshake sounds really good right now. What do you say, Helen? It's Halloween. Let's treat ourselves. Will you join me in a chocolate milkshake?"

He sensed her hesitation and slight fear. He pulled back slightly and quietly proceeded, "Or perhaps at this point you're too afraid to even talk to me." He studied her eyes, desperately seeking some cordiality. "You must really think I'm crazy or at the very least a silly old man." He laughed nervously and looked at her with a look of fervent hope.

The wheels behind Helen's eyes were turning. Her tears began to dry as she searched her memory for something once said to her. She closed her eyes and tried to get very quiet, so she could hear them.

Helen, if I have to turn the universe inside out, I will find you. If I have to pass through a hundred lifetimes, I will do it to find you. I may be an old man and you may be an old woman. You may not recognize me by the time it happens, but you will know and I will know, because nothing can separate us.

David's resolute promise came flooding back to her from so many years ago on that sunny day as they lay on the grass by the river. He had hovered over her so determined to make her understand that nothing would keep them apart.

"No," Helen suddenly said aloud.

"No?" the stranger said back with a very disappointed look. He straightened up and let go of Helen's arms. "No milkshake, huh?"

"I mean, no, I don't think you're a silly old man," said Helen.

A look of relief came over his face and they both laughed. He kept his gaze locked on hers. "Then a milkshake?" he asked.

"Yes, a milkshake sounds wonderful," she said, slowly drawing her mouth into a smile. She had no idea what was happening to her. It all seemed incredibly irrational, but she didn't really care. A peace swept over her like the first fresh breeze of spring.

The stranger extended his arm out for Helen to take as he said, "Well, then, Lady Helen, shall we?" She linked her arm in his as he escorted her into the café next door, where Helen's mother first met David's mother, all because of a tiny silver heart on a necklace.